JULIE CHAPPELL

Contrary Qualities of Elements

Short Stories

Fine Dog Press

WHERE GOOD BOOKS FIND A HOME

*For Evelyn, Cameron, and Saxon
in the hope that they hold together in lasting alliance.*

Contents

Preface

Note on the title of this collection—

The title translates a phrase from Geoffrey Chaucer's *Boece*, itself a translation (c. 1380-1387) of Boethius's *De Consolatio Philosophiae* (c. 524). In Chaucer's translation of Boethius' Book II, Prosa 8, Metrum 8, Lady Philosophy instructs Boethius, proclaiming in the verse portion, "that the contrarious qualites of elementz holden among hemself allyance perdurable" [that the contrary qualities of elements hold together among themselves in lasting alliance]. At the end of this verse, Lady Philosophy claims that humans could be happy if they were governed by the same force instead of by their inclinations, desires, and emotions.

Keeping Time

Keeping time, time, time,
In a sort of Runic rhyme,
To the pæan of the bells—
Of the bells
Edgar Allan Poe, "The Bells" (1848)

Alice adjusted the cheap plastic sunglasses on her eyes and covered her thinning hair with a brown scarf, her dress a simple shift as plain and brown as her scarf. She pulled on the old, tweed coat Mrs. Halsey had given her three years ago and went out the door, satisfied with her resemblance to the reclusive film star, Greta Garbo.

As a young girl, Alice had seen all of Garbo's movies. Saturday afternoon movies were what she lived for. Whenever she could earn fifteen cents running an errand for her neighbor, Mrs. Pettigrew, Alice would hide the money from her mother and sneak out on Saturdays to the movie theatre.

Garbo's loner image appealed to the little girl who had no father and whose mother lived in a fantasy she created about a life of wealth and privilege that she believed had been stolen from her. Her daughter disrupted her fantasy, constantly needing something, so she ignored the child as much as possible. Alice's desire for love never realized, she wished for a life outside the house she shared with her mother. Like

Garbo, she would seek to be left alone and content with that. Fate has a wicked way of gratifying wishes.

One day in late summer shortly after Alice's sixteenth birthday, Alice's mother screamed something about her appointed time having come and ran out into the street in front of the four o'clock bus. She died instantly.

Alice felt little or no emotion at her mother's death, but the charity extended to Alice by the Salvation Army and the attention given to her by the Women Helping Orphans was gratifying. Alice had never been so cared for. That duty of care lasted one week.

After that, no one bothered Alice when she decided to drop out of school or when she took the little money her mother had left in a drawer and moved out of the decrepit, three-room house into a cheap apartment over the downtown hardware store. At sixteen, she legally couldn't be forced to go to school and was nobody's burden of care.

The last day she was at her old house, Alice stepped out on the stoop with her mother's worn carpet bag filled with her own few clothes. She didn't bother to lock the door since there was nothing left worth stealing. She had already moved what little else she had to her small apartment. But as she turned to walk down the two steps, a scraggly, yellow kitten appeared howling and walking unsteadily toward her. Although she couldn't be certain that her heroine, Greta Garbo, kept a cat, Alice believed she might have. The little, female kitten was picked up and duly named Garbo. Her job at the Woolworth's lunch counter sustained her and her cat in their meagre existence.

Alice found a kind of desultory happiness performing the famous Garbo in the daytime while she walked to and from her job at Woolworth's. When the Salvation Army, who had given Alice some clothes after her mother was killed, asked Alice to ring their bell that Christmas, she had thought it a fine way to continue her disguise at night. She could even take her cat with her into the kettle hut, and the two would be alone in the crowds as Alice rang the bell from inside the hut.

One night just before Christmas that year, several boys from her former school recognized her in her hut and began teasing her first about her Garbo act and then about the circumstances of her "crazy" mother's death. Alice ignored them as best she could, and they soon tired of their game. A few minutes after they had walked away, one boy in a bright red, plaid jacket returned.

He shuffled his feet in front of Alice's hut as he mumbled an apology. Then he asked her to meet him behind the old theatre when she finished that night. He promised to give her something to prove his apology was genuine. Alice's curiosity and loneliness urged her to agree to meet him.

She finished her shift ringing the bell and sorting the odd "I Like Ike" and "All the Way with Adlai" buttons out of the coins so the kettle with the day's takings would be ready when the Captain made his rounds. After that, she locked her hut, picked up Garbo, and headed for the alley that ran behind the buildings on the main drag.

The oldest theatre in town had closed two years before while the owners raised enough money to repair the walls and bring the electricity up to code. When Alice neared the back of that building, she noticed the scaffolding and some wooden pallets with bricks and buckets of mortar that the workmen had left on the site. No street lamp shed any light on this section of the alley.

She stopped a few feet away from the scaffolding, "Danny?"

No one answered. Feeling a trick coming on, she turned to leave with the cat squirming in her arms. Garbo was becoming a handful, having grown quickly with proper care and love. As Alice held tightly to Garbo while trying to turn back toward her apartment, she heard the boy's voice.

"Alice. I'm over here at the back, by the scaffolding."

"Come out here where I can see you," Alice countered from the darkness.

"Oh, come on, Alice. We've got more privacy back here," he wheedled. Alice hesitated then stepped slowly toward the sound of his voice. As she neared the scaffolding, she felt something hard and cold hit her right ear. A snowball, tightly packed, turned the sphere to solid ice. Before she could reverse course, several more ice balls hit around her head and shoulders. She could hear the excited laughter of several boys coming from nearby, but the fragments of the ice balls clinging to her face obscured what little she could see in the dark alley.

She had been trying desperately to hold onto her howling, wriggling cat, but the last icy projectile loosened Alice's grip on Garbo, who ran terrified down the alley. Alice cried out and began to run in the same direction as the cat. Suddenly, a car's headlights illuminated the scene in the alley.

Alice stopped, momentarily blinded by the lights. Then the car lights lurched to one side, the car narrowly missing the cat. Garbo disappeared at break-neck speed into the darkness beyond. The car backed quickly out of the alley and sped away.

Alice stood unmoving, holding her breath, leaning against one of the buildings. The boys, shouting at each other, took off from their hiding places, scattering in all directions. The boy who had tempted her there ran by Alice and tripped on the brick pallets and mortar buckets near the scaffolding. She put her hands up to cover her ears as the clanging and crashing of buckets and bricks exploded. Then, silence.

Alice remained flat against the building in the stillness for a few more minutes before stepping forward. Her eyes, more accustomed to the darkness now, allowed her to make her way down the alley to the spot where her cat had disappeared.

Garbo did not respond to Alice calling her, so she retraced her steps back to the scaffolding where she found the boy's prone body still lying among the scattered bricks and mortar buckets.

Is he dead, she wondered vaguely?

The north wind blew hard, the gusts swirling diverse patterns in the snow as Alice headed down main street toward her kettle hut in front of the department store. When she reached the hut, she drew a small key from her pocket and unlocked the door. She reached inside, pulled out the kettle and stand, and set these in front of her window. Satisfied at the placement of her kettle, Alice went back inside the hut, closing and locking the door behind her.

She adjusted her newly-acquired hat for maximum warmth. The Army also made sure she received warm gloves every Christmas so that her perpetually chapped hands wouldn't suffer as much from the cold as she rang the bell. She picked up her small, gold bell and waited.

The glass doors of the department store were directly across the sidewalk from her hut. On the far wall of the store was a large, round-faced clock, the clock and its hands just large enough for her to keep time. Alice peered through the glass doors. It was 4PM exactly. She began ringing her bell and replaying an old Garbo film in her head as a long-haired girl with a fringed jacket and a choker of beads tossed a few coins in Alice's kettle.

She continued ringing the bell, slowly and rhythmically with a distracted "Thank you" or "Merry Christmas" for those who dropped coins into the bucket. It was the Sunday before Christmas, and the crowd along the sidewalk as well as those going in and out of the store were ever increasing as night descended.

Alice watched the people with their sacks and packages, laughing and talking together, waving or offering Christmas greetings to others as they passed her by. Every now and then, the sound of the bell would cause them to look over at Alice as they stopped nearby to chat to each other or walked in the direction of the hut as they exited the store. Her own expression never changed, but someone would inevitably look guilty and walk over to throw some coins in Alice's red kettle.

"Hello, Alice, dear."

"Oh, hullo, Mrs. Halsey." Alice didn't want to disrupt Garbo's "Ninotchka," playing in her head, but Mrs. Halsey's offhand generosity to Alice over the years must be gratified by Alice's attention whenever it was demanded.

"How are our Christmas givers today, Alice?"

"Fine, Mrs. Halsey."

"Alice, where are your gloves?"

"Lost 'em," Alice lied. She had taken them off a few minutes before to blow her nose in her frayed handkerchief, and then got lost in her film.

"Well, here, Alice. I have an extra pair in my bag since I just bought some new ones to go with my new coat." Mrs. Halsey rummaged through her purse and retrieved a pair of red gloves, far too big for Alice.

"Thank you, Mrs. Halsey." Alice drew the gloves on as Mrs. Halsey watched, satisfied once more with her own generosity.

"Merry Christmas, dear." Mrs. Halsey flung some loose change from the bottom of her purse into Alice's bucket and scurried away.

Alice stared absently at the over-large red gloves swallowing her small hands before she pulled them off and put her other ones back on. They were warm and a good fit. She returned to the mechanical ringing of her bell as Ninotchka looked sternly at Count Leon.

At 9 o'clock, the department store began its closing rituals. A few minutes later, the lights went out. As Alice began *her* nightly rituals, she found only a handful of Nixon and McGovern buttons among the coins, a handmade button that read: "Don't Change Dicks in the Middle of a Screw Vote for Nixon in '72." Alice tossed it in the trash, feeling only relief that she could close up her kettle hut and go home.

The snow had been falling steadily throughout her shift in the hut, making walking difficult along the snow-swept sidewalks. Only a few merry makers, coming out of closing restaurants along the main street, disturbed Alice's peace.

She put her hands into her coat pockets seeking whatever added warmth she could. When she reached the stairway in the alley that led up to her apartment above the hardware store, Alice started the slow climb up the metal steps. Over the last few months as she grew heavier from inactivity and indifference to her meagre diet, Alice had found the steps more and more tiring.

I'm thirty-six, she thought, remembering Mrs. Halsey's small present last year on her 35^h birthday. Mrs. Halsey had made quite a spectacle of giving it to Alice at the Woolworth's lunch counter. Alice cringed at the memory of the satisfied smirk of the old woman as Alice dutifully opened the little package with one cotton handkerchief inside.

Finally in her apartment, Alice sat down in the worn, chintz chair by the door without taking off coat or gloves.

I'll take these off in a minute, she told herself. Instead, she continued to sit in the chair.

The little table next to her held one item, a photograph set in a cheap, plastic frame with curling leaves and flowers running along the sides. The green and yellow of leaves and flowers were much faded now, but this was the only photograph Alice ever possessed. Mrs. Halsey had snapped a picture of Alice holding Garbo, the two framed by the window of the kettle hut that first Christmas after her mother died. Alice gazed at the photo until she fell asleep, coat and gloves still in place.

Early Christmas morning, she woke to loud banging and crashing noises from the alley behind her building. She sat up in the chair trying to break the heavy fog of uncomfortable sleep and hunger pangs from eating no supper the night before. She tried to remember what day of the week it was to help her place the noise.

Not trash day, she thought. *It's Christmas day. Last night was my last night in my hut until next year. That's right.*

It took Alice a few minutes to heave herself up from the chair. When she did, she walked across the room to peer out the window onto the alley below. But the glass on the window was steamed over from age and poor workmanship, a layer of ice framing the Impressionist scene. Alice took the ball of her still-gloved palm and rubbed a clear spot in the center of the glass.

She could just make out workmen knocking bricks from an outside wall halfway down the alley from her building.

Why are they working on Christmas, she wondered?

Alice descended the easier inside stairs to the ground floor and unlocked the back door of the closed hardware store. She stepped out the door into the alley. As she stared down the alley, she could see the workmen and some gawkers gathered nearby what was now the wreckage of the back wall of the old theatre.

Alice moved toward the crowd. As she drew closer, she heard the exclamations of the people staring into the rubble and shuffled along the edge of the crowd. She stopped near the debris of the partially demolished wall.

One man was talking loudly to make sure his audience could hear his pronouncements. "Poor kid, musta ran in and got stuck behind a half-rebuilt wall. But who woulda bricked him up finishing the wall? Them renovations was some twenty years ago. A crew from Chicago or somewheres else did that job. None of us locals was invited."

A few people around him nodded as they ghoulishly gaped at the skeleton of an adolescent boy, pieces of red plaid clothing hanging from his boney cavity.

Alice turned and walked away. The truth secured inside.

An Ill Wind

The staccato bass vibration of the outboard motor shattered the peace of the lake and scattered the wintering pelicans, floating and fishing on its surface.

A solitary figure silhouetted against the muted grey of the lake sat in a small motorboat keeping his face, like his craft, pointing due west. He didn't seem to notice the agitated birds swirling around his trajectory. Living things were meaningless to a man with a body in his boat.

Standing with her camera on the bench encircling her open deck, Norah had been shooting a series of close-ups of the dozen or so white pelicans in her part of the lake. Disrupted by the abrupt, fluttering exit of the pelicans and the unexpected sound of the motorboat, the usual rush of contempt for human intrusion into the habitat she shared with the lake and forest creatures surged through her.

This time, she told herself, I'm going to send a complaint, and, if I didn't spoil it, a picture of the offending human and his assault weapon.

The next moment a strangely warm, late November wind roared like a breaking wave through the trees. The wind gained momentum as it kicked up leaves from the ground and tore the remaining leaves from the late autumn branches of Blackjack and Pin Oak. An added punch came from a gust so strong it nearly pitched Norah off the bench. She only just managed to keep her balance and step onto the floor of the deck. A tumble down the steep cliff to the shoreline along the forest floor at sunset could be fatal.

Her struggle with the wind momentarily tamped down her righteous anger at the intruding boater. Then she spotted her former subjects silhouetted against the darkening sky, flying into the cove opposite her place, out of range. Frustrated, Norah retreated to the quiet of her house with her dog, a Blue Heeler-Aussie mix, trotting along beside her.

Two years ago, Norah was asked by a friend to organize a photo shoot and website set-up for the local animal shelter to increase visibility for the animals. She quickly fell in love with an active and charming six-week old puppy, whose intellect and dark-fur-outlined eyes reminded Norah of the smart, bespectacled girl of the Scooby gang, Velma, who, like Norah's new puppy, eagerly sniffed out clues.

Like most herding dogs, Velma instinctively knew when to be silent and watch and when to sound the alarm. Of course, her natural herding instincts were constantly thwarted with no cows or sheep to drive. That meant the various nocturnal creatures, especially raccoons and opossum, nightly sauntering across the upper deck, would set the dog racing in the house along the glass wall while the intruders remained out of reach.

Since Norah abhorred fences, none existed on her place. Velma's natural instincts to corral and pursue vagrant wildlife would be unrestrained. Consequently, Norah began training her dog to respond to voice and hand signals when Velma was only ten weeks old.

Still, Velma stood sentinel most evenings watching the deck, forest, and lake that stretched out beyond their house. Those interloping raccoons and opossum, flaunting their trespass, would have her to answer to.

Inside the house after the disturbance of the motorboat, Norah put the kettle on for tea and fed Velma. Then she made herself a pot of warming, relaxing, egg drop soup with spinach and ginger. But even as she prepared her soup, the noisome disturbance of the motorboat still grated on her. She chopped the spinach a bit too vigorously, yelping in surprise as the blade nicked her flesh.

Velma raised her head from her bowl along with an eyebrow.

"Sorry, Vel. I'm still suffering from that motorized invader." Norah took a deep breath and continued chopping.

The tragedy of the virus now keeping the country in lockdown had quieted the lake. The state repeatedly extended the ban on using public boat ramps, recently prohibiting all boat traffic until further notice. Without the noise of boats and people, the pandemic silence of the lake proved a boon to Norah's work. She felt guilty about that.

So, how did that nuisance of a boater get on the lake, she wondered?

Norah's light meal over, she went to her study with her camera to see if any of her afternoon photo shoot was viable. Her study on the south side of the house had no windows to distract her. She could let herself be thoroughly consumed by her work in such a space.

Some of the day's photos captured the light reflecting off the water in such a way that the pelicans' feathers appeared like gossamer, floating, mimicking the silky webs of the small grey spiders that tried each year between spring and winter to take over Norah's deck.

Norah kept advancing through the images on her camera until the last one. She thought that she had jerked the camera away too abruptly when the discomfiting noise of the man in the boat upended her shoot, but she was mistaken. Her screen revealed a well-focused image of a man heading into the sunset, seemingly in pursuit of a squadron of pelicans.

I wonder if I can blow this up enough to reveal his face. The sunset array of pink and blue stripes across the western sky could enhance or, potentially, blur the details. At higher resolution, I might at least get a registration number or the name of the boat, if it has one.

She reversed through the photos to the start of the day's shoot before turning her camera off and setting it aside. Norah wanted to get a draft of her complaint done while the incident was still fresh in her mind.

She would copy it into the form available from the local Army Corps of Engineers website since that group claimed responsibility for monitoring all aspects of safety on the lake. Sending the information in an email to the state officials, who control public access for water craft, could bolster her complaint. If either or both had a portal for downloading images as well as documents, she would send the last photo, too.

When he got up that morning, Jackson felt optimistic about the upcoming visit from his former co-worker and would-be friend, Ben, later that day. He didn't like Ben but had tolerated him. The isolation though had made him agree to the visit.

They hadn't seen each other since their tech company used the pandemic as an excuse to downsize. Even though other people belligerently left their quarantine in early summer, Jackson hadn't needed the excuse of his lifelong, though now minor, asthma to stay away from Ben, if given a choice. 'I'm too much at risk, Dude', Jackson would claim when Ben called with some scheme to get together.

The lockdown allowed their former employer to push executives and middle management types to work online while a handful of warehouse staff remained on-site to sort inventory and ship product. In-store sales clerks with less than ten years service, like Jackson and Ben, were made redundant by the first of April.

Ben claimed that he had been preparing for just such a crisis for years. "I studied the history. We were due for some calamity sooner or later. I've been stockpiling TP, paper towels, wipes, sanitizer, other necessities for a long time, long before it was a thing," he bragged to Jackson.

A long time, my ass, Jackson thought, but kept that comment to himself. He knew Ben was indulging in some essential, for Ben, exaggeration. At the time, Jackson let Ben pat himself on the back, remembering quite clearly the moment in early February when Jackson caught Ben covertly listening to some executives talking about the potential crisis. When confronted about this, Ben stubbornly asserted that it was his own brilliant insight years before that triggered his survival instinct.

"Survival of the shiftiest," Jackson grumbled at the time, while enduring another onslaught of Ben's self-aggrandizement.

Ben also regularly attempted to one-up Jackson, who suspected Ben somehow cheated in his questionably high monthly sales figures at work. And his uncanny Fantasy Football wins were suspect. Ben never failed to crow about all of his 'victories', as he called them.

Since Jackson now lived on one of the state's biggest lakes, Ben maneuvered the conversation yesterday so that he could 'get out of the damn city for awhile'. Jackson relented since that would give him home field advantage in dealing with Ben. And a bit of human contact.

Yet, less than thirty minutes after Ben arrived the next afternoon, Jackson's usual irritation at the man's posturing and boasting peaked. He was only surprised at how little time it had taken. From the moment Ben walked through the door, he couldn't stop gushing over himself and his amazing prowess at his new passion, online gambling. Ben claimed to have made a fortune so far that year playing blackjack online, his PayPal account bursting with cash, or so he said.

Jackson smiled and nodded as Ben ratcheted on. Jackson was certain that seven months of post-lay-off quarantine, along with his sanity and his savings giving out, were responsible for his agreeing to Ben's annoying presence. Nothing else could explain his allowing Ben to come out to his place for a whole afternoon and evening.

When Jackson could finally get a word in, he asked Ben if he'd found a new job. Instead of a direct answer, Ben placed one finger by his nose and said nothing.

All these months not having to stare at his smug face and listen to his bullshit had been the upside of the lockdown, Jackson realized. I only answered the phone yesterday because he had been calling every day for three or four days. Curiosity kills.

In the looming darkness of the lake and surrounding woods, Jackson opened his eyes, before sitting up on the bench encircling the fire pit. With only coals glowing in the chimenea, Jackson peered into the darkness. Ben was not on the bench or anywhere in view.

He must have gone home when I passed out, Jackson thought as he blinked his eyes against the darkness. But I didn't have *that much* to drink. Three beers, maybe, and a glass of that cheap wine Ben brought?

Scrolling through his memory of the afternoon and evening, Jackson recalled his efforts to get Ben out of the house and onto the deck, a structure made up of ten wooden pallets lashed together. During the afternoon, Ben's increasingly intoxicated, non-stop chatter had proved too much. Jackson needed air.

He could almost conjure an image of himself sitting opposite Ben on the bench around the chimenea. Gravel covered the ground around the base of the fire pot, with Jackson's purpose-built wooden bench close enough but not too close to the chimenea. Next came flashes of an argument about something.

Jackson pulled on his hair trying to think. Fantasy Football?

Ben and Jackson started playing the game after a co-worker invited them to join his group of players about five years ago. To the new group's chagrin and Jackson's mortification, Ben nearly always won the pool at the end. The pandemic lay-offs at the company scattered the players and dampened their enthusiasm for fantasy play. No one wanted to restart the group when the season began in fall 2020. Jackson remembered Ben disparaging the game and its players and saying, 'Anyone who still plays is a loser'. Jackson dug deeper. The next memory he could tease out was Ben walking to his car to get something. But what?

Norah prepared for bed as usual after drafting her short narrative, downloading the day's digital photos to her webpage, and writing up notes for her weekly blog. For seven years before the lockdown, she had traveled around the state capturing elements of the natural world in all seasons and selling her photos to individuals, even to the state's tourism office. Norah enhanced her web presence every year, adding a weekly blog this year to offer a story behind each photo displayed for that week. The pandemic propelled more people online, and Norah's business boomed even as the cause desecrated the world around her. The guilt she felt tainted her good fortune. But Velma's need for activity kept Norah distracted from too much depressing introspection.

As with all humans sharing their lives with a dog, Norah and Velma spent as much time as possible outside. Norah kept the pup in voice range, especially at night. If Velma was going to encounter raccoons, opossum or the rarer bobcats, it would happen after dark.

When they came back in the house that night, Norah did her usual security check—deadbolt on the front door, locks secured on the two sliding doors lakeside. After that, she turned off all the lights and padded into her room, Velma close on her heels.

Norah flipped the light switch in her bathroom and stood in front of the extra large mirror over the sink. The size of the mirror allowed her not only to see her own reflection but that of a portion of her deck through the all-glass north wall behind her. The spectacular view of forest and lake from the deck in the daytime was worth any momentary qualm at the near impenetrable darkness of the forest at night. In the day, she could watch the birds and squirrels on the feeders and the water fowl on the lake or follow the progress of the storms approaching from the north.

In her bedroom, a Japanese-inspired screen blocked a portion of the glass wall. She claimed the artistry of the screen sold it. Nothing to do with shutting out the darkness while she slept. And Norah slept peacefully with Velma on the end of her bed.

In the morning, she would reread the draft of her complaint about the intruding boat and send it off. Then she and Velma would take their morning walk. Norah intended to go along the eastern edge of her property and down the cliff to the lakeshore. That way, she could get some early winter shots of lake and shoreline.

Jackson was still sitting on the bench working backward through his memory when he heard a boat motoring close-by. He recognized the sound as that of his own boat.

Did that moron take my boat out while he was drunk? I'll kick his ass for sure this time. Jackson's anger bounced through the trees as he stood up and walked toward the edge of the woods.

The cliffside was dense with trees and sloped down abruptly from the small weedy area between his cabin and the edge of the forest. The trees were nearly bare at this time of year with thousands of leaves covering the forest floor.

Walking through the thicket of trees, living and dead, Jackson needed to go slowly. His head was aching, and he didn't want to switch on the lantern he held in his hand. The light might give Ben advance warning of Jackson's arrival and give Ben a chance to conjure an excuse for taking the boat.

Jackson knew by the sound under his feet when he stepped onto his path of wood shavings. Although the red-brown cedar presented no contrast to the nearly identical colors of the fallen leaves, the sound of it crunching underfoot was distinctly different from that of the fallen leaves. As he made his way down the path, the increasing volume of the churning waves breaking on the shore offered a natural GPS for his trek down the cliff.

At the end of the path, the lake stretched out in front of him. At this spot, the Corps had given permission for Jackson to build a small ramp and dock for his boat. He switched on his lantern and stepped gingerly onto the ramp. A fall into the cold water would be a disadvantage in confronting Ben. But, the circle of lantern light did not spotlight Ben. Instead, it revealed an image Jackson couldn't quite get his head around.

The ground in front of the ramp to the dock had been thoroughly disordered by something. And darkly stained.

He lowered the lantern until the light illuminated only the area of disturbance. As he brought his head down closer to inspect it, he jumped back abruptly.

"Blood! It smells like blood," Jackson blurted aloud while the metallic smell of the blood ignited a pitch and roll in his stomach.

Once he stopped retching, Jackson stood up and raked his hands through his hair. As he did, he felt a bump on the back of his own head. Setting the lantern on the ground, he put his hands in its light. No blood. But his head was pounding and the muscles in his neck were stiffening.

At that moment, he heard movement through the woods behind him. Heavier than the usual curiosity seekers, the raccoons who came around every night looking for food or mischief.

I thought cougars didn't come through this area anymore. Maybe, that's why it's all bloody here. A cougar killed something and dragged it off. Yeah, but who drove your boat just now, dumbass? As he berated himself, the hairs on the back of his neck began to tingle.

It was all he could do to keep himself steady and quiet. Jackson squinted trying to see further into the trees. No one or no thing was there, at least not as far as he could tell. He noticed that the dark was receding slightly as dawn pushed into the night, but the extra light only created moving shadows in the dense woods.

"Ben, are you there?" he called out as he scrambled from ramp to dock to boat.

Standing in the boat, Jackson tried to calm down, to shake off the creeping sensation that crawled up his back and head. The cold wind coming off the lake wasn't helping. He shivered and reached down into the boat's storage compartment to retrieve the yellow windbreaker he always kept there. As his hand closed over the jacket, he realized it was wadded up.

"What the hell! I always fold this neatly before I put it away. What the fuck? Ben, you asshole!" he cried, pulling the jacket out of the compartment. The jacket felt warm in his hand.

The chill climbing up his spine intensified, and he leapt out of the boat onto the dock. He felt rattled. But the cause of his rising panic was complicated. His body decided what to do before his mind could comply. He jumped off the dock and ran.

Velma's low growl woke Norah from a strange dream where boats were running amuck on the lake as she frantically tried to focus her camera on one. She sat up, Velma continuing her throaty growl.

"Velma, quiet."

The dog slid deftly off the bed and stood completely still in front of the Japanese screen. Norah tossed the covers back and sat for a few seconds on the edge of the bed to clear her head. She listened, too, but heard nothing. Then Velma began to growl in earnest just as a loud thud sounded on the deck.

"What—" Norah cut her involuntary response short. The clouds parted long enough for a full moon to illuminate the deck and through the translucent screen could make out a blur of tawny and black whizzing by. Velma barked and ran along the glass wall keeping pace with the creature on the other side.

"Velma, leave it."

Velma stopped abruptly in the living room while staring out the glass wall and grumbling. The apparition had vanished.

"Come here, girl. You don't want to tangle with a bobcat. Strange, they usually avoid inhabited places. Why was it running so fast? What could have spooked it. A dog? Another bobcat? A loose human?"

Norah flipped on the deck lights and stared through the living room glass, patting her dog's head to calm them both. No creature appeared at either end of the deck. She considered walking out to peer over the railing but thought better of it. Instead, she switched off the lights and went back down the hallway to bed.

The adrenaline rush caused by the flying bobcat left a buzz, making it unlikely that Norah would get back to sleep. After tossing and turning for a while, she checked her phone. 6:35AM.

What could have stirred a bobcat to run at such speed across the deck, she wondered? Only four other houses within a football field of mine and those are summer places, she mused. No other full-time residents. The summer folks rarely return to the lake in winter, though whenever they do, their untended dogs generally wreak havoc among the wildlife.

Norah fumed at yet another human transgression of manners practiced by the inconsiderate city dwellers, oblivious to the need for boundaries in the countryside to preserve flora and fauna as well as neighborly peace and harmony.

As the faintest bit of daylight highlighted the Japanese screen, Velma began to whine. She couldn't get back to sleep either. Norah got up, dressed, and folded the screen to one side. Velma leapt off the bed anxiously waiting for Norah to open the door.

The two walked out onto the deck and turned toward the east railing where Norah had cut a gate for easy access to the area of native grasses that she had planted on top of the cliff. Velma bolted down the few steps to the ground as soon as Norah unlatched the gate. The dog sniffed her way to the edge of the forest while Norah stayed on the deck, pulling her long sweater more tightly around her in an attempt to ward off the sharp northeast wind.

As soon as she saw Velma rise from her squat, Norah called her in. "Come on, you. It's getting colder by the minute. Let's have our breakfast. I need a cup of tea!"

Always ready for her breakfast, Velma bounded up the few stairs onto the deck. As Norah latched the gate behind them, she caught a glimpse of movement down by the lake through the nearly leafless trees.

The predawn darkness slowed Jackson down as he ran mindlessly west, having to dodge the outcropping of giant rock formations along the rocky shore. Twice he tripped and fell, jumped up, and kept running. The third time he slipped on a fairly sizable chunk of rock protruding like a root from the enormous mother lode, the colossal boulders rising twenty or more feet above his head. The fall sent him sprawling onto a mass of baseball-sized gravel, littering the shoreline. This time, there was no jumping up.

Momentarily stunned, Jackson felt the warm liquid trickling down over his right eye, his cheek. He tried to push himself up but couldn't. His body was vibrating.

After a few minutes, he could stand. Where was I running to or who was I running from, he wondered? Jackson leaned against the wall of the mother lode.

The bright yellow windbreaker was still in his hand so he put it on without thinking about who might have warmed it earlier. With one arm, he swiped at the blood dripping from his eye and down his cheek onto the jacket. His action smeared blood on the sleeve. He continued resting against the rock wall for several more minutes. As the sun crested in the east, Jackson eased himself off the outcropping and began laboriously retracing his steps.

The early morning sun glistening off the water made it more difficult for Norah to detect what was moving through the trees below. She shifted position on the deck until she could be sure the object was a person clad in bright yellow, too near where she'd left her canoe. The yellow triggered her memory and her anger at yesterday's intruding boatman.

"And *now* you are trespassing! And my canoe's not yet put up for the winter. Damn." As she spoke, Norah started moving toward the deck gate with Velma close behind.

Jackson's head was still muddled. He squinted against the sun in his eyes. As he did, he felt a sharp pain stab through the right side of his head. He let out an involuntary but loud grunt.

The sound momentarily stopped Norah and Velma's progress down the slope. "Like the croaking of a coot, Velma. But coots don't wear yellow jackets."

Now Norah and Velma were moving swiftly down their well-kept path to the lake, thinking to intercept the yellow jacket, hoping it didn't have a stinger.

When they reached the end of her path, she shouted, "Hey, what are you doing there?"

Hearing her own voice, she realized that she hadn't thought to grab a mask. Why would she when she had only meant to take the dog out? She would have to keep her distance, but Velma would not.

"What?" Jackson threw a glance up the shore, where a woman and a dog emerged, blocking his way.

"Stop. What are you doing here? I know the Corps' easement is not officially my property, but everything above here is mine. And private. No trespassing." The Blue Heeler in Velma's DNA took over when she heard Norah's voice take on a certain note. The dog moved between Norah and Jackson growling, edging toward him, staring him down.

"Call off your dog, please. I, I, went for a walk from my place before daybreak and, and lost track of where I was. That's all."

"You're bleeding all over that yellow jacket."

"Yeah, well, I fell over a boulder and gashed my head. No big deal," hoping to convince himself as well as Norah.

"Where do you live?" Skepticism rife.

"Down that way," he pointed east.

"Really? I've lived here a long time. No houses down there. Only several empty lots. Do you have a trailer or something on a lot?"

The classist sneer he detected in her voice irritated Jackson. "No. I built a log cabin last fall."

"I see," she conceded, calling Velma to her side.

"I'll head back to my place now, *if* you don't mind."

She didn't like his tone but stepped back onto her path well out of his way. Velma stayed between Norah and the yellow jacket until he rounded the bend of the peninsula.

Back inside the house, Norah fixed Velma's breakfast and gave her an extra biscuit treat for being such a 'good dog'. As she prepared her own food, Norah couldn't help wondering what the man in the blood-stained yellow jacket had been doing when he was illegally driving a boat the day before and again today walking along the lake too near her property in the early morning hours. But she would find out.

"I need to send in my complaint along with that photo, if possible. Then, we'll break our no-contact code and pay a neighborly visit on that man, eh Velma?" Norah bit vigorously into her bagel.

Jackson reached his dock fuming. But then the last hours came roaring back to him as he saw his boat starting to drift away from the dock.

"Fuck!"

Jackson waded into the cold water up to his waist. Then he pulled the boat to the dock holding tightly to the rope while he climbed out to tie it down.

He really didn't know what to do next. He couldn't sort his emotions any more, feeling only confusion and wondering what would happen to him, to his life after his friend's probable boat theft and then disappearance. Did anyone else know Ben was coming to Jackson's?

Yes, Jackson thought, we'd been drinking and I passed out. I woke up…when? This morning? Ben, nowhere in sight? Blood all over the shore by the dock, the boat out on the lake and yet returned to its own dock.

Had I told Ben that I kept my boat keys on a hook in the kitchen? Did he take them walking to his car? If not Ben, who else was here to take the boat out? Where the fuck is Ben? And whose blood is on the ground? Ben's?

Still dazed by the minor head injury from the fall and all the questions making it worse, Jackson finally walked back up the cliffside to his cabin.

Norah and Velma hiked slowly, deliberately down the last fifty feet of road where Jackson now sat in an old rocker on the small front porch of his cabin.

"You can turn around and go back to your own place. This is PRIVATE PROPERTY!" He shouted, struggling for self-control, as he hoisted himself out of the chair.

"I'm sorry about this morning, but I was afraid you were after my canoe. I ran out of energy after a long day of paddling and shooting before it turned too cold. I set the canoe halfway up the slope, upside down under a big cedar intending to retrieve it today."

She hadn't intended to do more than offer a semi-sincere apology. Not reveal so much about her activities with the canoe. At least she didn't tell him that she was going to hang the canoe under the rafters from hooks on the side of her house.

"I have a boat. Don't need your damn canoe. You shoot?" Worried.

"Photographs. Digital ones. It's my profession." Almost pleasant.

Relief and irritation. "Well, at least you have a job." Unnecessary info for this nosy, pushy woman.

"Oh, I'm sorry." So many people had lost their jobs since the pandemic hit, she felt guilty again.

"Yeah, well. As soon as this shit blows over, I'll be back to work. You need to go home now."

Norah thought he was being too aggressive, considering she had apologized. Twice. Velma stood quiet beside her mistress but never took her eyes off Jackson.

"Your dog's freakin' me out. Can you just go?" He glared at Norah but never looked directly at the dog.

"Fine. I just wanted to see that you were alright. Your bleeding seems to have stopped." She stared at him now, like the dog, he thought. Piercing his head, teasing out his thoughts. Maybe she could tell him what they were.

He considered shouting at her again but thought better of it. Instead, he turned and walked into his cabin without a word and without looking back.

Norah didn't trust this 'new' neighbor. The construction debris across from his cabin wasn't the only mess on this lot. She and Velma watched him go into his cabin before they trudged back up the road toward home.

The unexpected visit of the obviously snooping woman and her dog unnerved Jackson. He sat down on his couch trying to focus.

It was the mask, he thought. You can see the eyes but not really the expression. Her eyes wide, staring, like the dog's, intense, freakish, x-ray vision boring through you.

Jackson shook his head trying to clear the image, thinking, Ben's cell phone. He always has it with him. Why didn't I think of that sooner? Just call Ben and see why his car's still here and *he's* not.

"Shit." He always put his phone down on the coffee table when he came home. But, it's not there now, only a couple of used plastic beer cups.

Jackson began a frantic search for his phone. Twenty minutes later, he ran outside to see if he had carried it to the bench around the chimenea. He searched on and under the bench and then around the whole area.

No phone. Then he had a thought that made his stomach pitch and roll again. But this time no vomiting, only churning anger.

"Did that bastard Ben take *my* phone?"

Then Jackson started back down his path until he reached the dock. Averting his eyes from the bloody mess near his ramp, he clambered onto it and then the dock. His phone must have fallen out when he'd leaned over the storage compartment in the dark.

He began searching. In the storage compartment, the shelf near the steering wheel, and finally on his knees to scour the boat's floor. No phone.

"Dammit, Ben. Why the fuck did you take my phone and my boat? And where are you?"

In the house again, Jackson saw how badly he had trashed his house as he searched for his phone. Then came a knock at the door.

"If it's that annoying woman and her damned dog, snooping around again, I'll—" he muttered walking in a fury toward his front door still in his blood-stained yellow jacket.

"I thought I—"

"Excuse me, Mr.—?" a masked man in a uniform stepped back another few feet away from the unmasked man at the door.

"Wha— Beckwith. My name is Jackson Beckwith. Who are you?" Jackson failing in his attempt at nonchalance.

"I'm a ranger for the state park that includes this lake. We've had a report that you were out in your boat on the lake yesterday evening. Did you know that there is a boat ban on, and has been since April?" The ranger's eyes moved quickly over the bloody jacket and then focused on Jackson's face.

"Yes, of course," Jackson began but then remembered that his boat *had* been on the lake—without him. "My friend took the boat out."

"You should have told him no boats on the lake. Since it's your boat, I'll have to write you up." The ranger pulled a pad and pen from inside his quilted jacket and began to write.

"Fine. Whatever."

"Sir, this is a serious infraction and may well result in your boat being impounded, your dock being dismantled, and a substantial fine, at the very least." No holes barred and unsmiling.

"But I lost my job and, oh, nevermind," Jackson sighed and leaned against the door jamb while the ranger again eyed the bloody jacket, before turning his attention back to writing on his pad.

After answering more questions and showing several documents to the ranger, including his boat registration, his driver's license, and his boat and car insurance cards, Jackson asked, "Is that all?"

"For now." The ranger walked back to his Jeep while Jackson closed the door.

Jackson failed to see the ranger get into his vehicle and pick up his two-way radio handset.

Twenty minutes later, the police arrived with sirens blaring.

Velma's sharp canine hearing picked up the sirens first. When the dog started to howl, Norah listened for the source.

"Sirens. Not fire trucks, but more than one vehicle. Getting closer."

Norah and Velma watched the top of the hill from her driveway and saw the cop cars
heading down away from her place.

"The police are turning onto the road to that man's cabin. I knew something was up with him. Definitely a dodgy character."

When the police officers knocked on Jackson's door, he wanted to run out the back and along the shore again. But he gathered himself together and opened the door.

"If this is about the boat ban business, I've already had a visit from the state park ranger, and—" stop talking, you idiot.

"We had a call from the ranger, but it's not about the boat ban, exactly," said one of the cops taking charge now. "What happened to your jacket and your face?"

"Nothing, I, well, I walked along the shoreline this morning, at, before sunrise and fell over some rocks." Jackson's angst was reasserting itself.

"Can you show us where that happened?" Another cop smiled but not in a friendly way.

"Yeah, sure." Jackson imagined bolting out the back door again.

The three cops followed Jackson through the house, blatantly looking around as they did. They kept the pace slow. Jackson's urge to run tamped down as he remembered that every criminal in a cop show who took off running, was caught, *and* prosecuted.

Once the group cleared the trees, two of the cops forged ahead toward the dock, stopping up short at the sight of the blood on the shore.

"There are no rocks here but plenty more blood than a cut over your eye could produce," sneered one.

Within an hour, the area had been cordoned off, forensics had arrived and scoured the bloodied shore, ramp and dock, and Jackson's boat had been towed away. Jackson was taken in for questioning.

No, he didn't need a lawyer. Yet.

About two hours later, cops showed up at Norah's door and started asking questions.

Did she know her neighbor down the other way on this road? No. *Did she hear or see anything the night before or this morning?* Only a bobcat. Shortly after, saw the man in a yellow jacket with blood on it. He said he fell, and he was bleeding fairly steadily from a gash over his right eye. *What time was that?* 7ish this morning. *Where was that?* At the bottom of my path through the forest to the lake. *Did he account for his presence there on your property?* It's the Army Corps of Engineer's easement but, yes, he said he had taken a walk before dawn and tripped over one of the outcroppings, hitting his head on a large rock. *Did he seem angry or disturbed in any way?* Well, confused, perhaps, and a bit aggressive when I told him that he was dangerously close to trespassing on my property. I have an expensive canoe that hadn't yet been hauled up for winter. *Did you think he was trying to steal it?* At first. *Why did you decide he wasn't after your canoe?* He wasn't headed up the slope when I confronted him. I also didn't know he had bought one of the lots east of here. *If you think of anything else, give us a call, okay?* Of course.

She took the officer's card before he walked out the door.

The police took the jacket and placed it in a plastic evidence bag as soon as they brought him into the station and made him repeat in an endless loop just how he had gotten the cut over his eye. Then they coaxed him into giving a DNA sample. 'Just to eliminate you from the inquiry' before running his name through their criminal database. No serious criminal activities appeared, only a speeding ticket from 2019.

The search team at his place found two empty wine bottles, a dozen beer cans, and a pizza box from the convenience store on the highway. No weapons of any kind. Apparently, Ben's car, still at his cabin when the police arrived, had been included in the search warrant. Jackson saw that Ben's car was gone when the police finally took Jackson home around 1AM. His head was throbbing. He popped the top on a bottle of ibuprofen and downed four with a shot of whiskey. Then he fell into bed.

When Velma whined for her bedtime outing the next night, Norah was deep in thought. But, having earlier changed into her sleep sweats, she had only to pull on a long sweater to take Velma outside.

Fifteen minutes later, Velma's cold nose touched Norah's hand, stirring her from her reverie as she stared through the mass of empty winter trees wondering about her neighbor and the cops.

"What were you doing in your boat evening before last? Is it connected to your being on the shore in front of my place early the next morning? Should I take this photo to the cops to see who they think it is?" Norah wondered aloud.

Velma's low growl interrupted her musings.

"What is it, girl? I know you're ready to go in and—" Then Norah heard it, too.

She signaled Velma's silence. The two walked into the main part of the house, deck and house now in nearly complete darkness. The only light, the tiny blue glow framing Velma's water fountain in the corner of the living room.

Even in the dark, Norah's progress would be sure unless Velma suddenly launched herself at something on the other side of the glass wall. But the dog stayed with her human step for step.

"Did I forget to bring in the bird seed bag? I was pretty distracted this morning, Velma. Stay." As she spoke, she switched all the deck lights on.

The extremely fat raccoon, momentarily stunned by the light, froze, then scurried over to the west edge of the deck where it jumped off. Velma vibrated and wriggled in place with her nose pressed against the glass wall.

"I knew it. Darn raccoons always looking for something to pilfer. Let's go out on the deck and shoo him further away, Velma. But stay with me!"

Norah only had to crack the slider wide enough for Velma to get through before the dog ran barking in the direction she had last seen the raccoon.

"Velma!"

The dog stopped running and barking, and Norah walked over to the railing of the upper deck to try to penetrate the darkness of the forest. The floodlight on that side of the deck was aimed toward the woods but gave only a few feet of illumination into the trees. Norah couldn't see the raccoon or any other creature on the ground. But she heard something moving through the leaves on the forest floor.

At first, she thought it might be the raccoon or a opossum disturbed by the raccoon's flight. The heavy displacement of leaves, started, then stopped, then started again. Was it animal or human? I've never seen a cougar come through here though people claim they do from time to time.

Norah opened the slider again and signaled Velma into the house. As she did, she reached her hand inside and flipped off the lights, but she stayed on the deck and stepped quietly toward the east end. Velma followed along on the inside of the glass wall.

At that end of her deck, a recessed area with a concrete floor created a space for Norah to store her gardening implements and other tools on a purpose-built wooden shelf. Next to that on one side, bags of potting soil, greensand, and manure leaned against one of two cedar-planked outside walls of the house. A heavy-duty shovel for digging in the hard clay soil hung on the other side of the shelving.

Norah didn't need any light to know precisely where to reach for her shovel. Soundlessly, she wrested it from its bracket on the wall. When the movement in the leaves ceased, Norah pulled herself into the empty space between the shelving and the corner where the two cedar walls met.

Jackson's mind had been fragmenting ever since the ordeal with the cops the day before. "Fucking Ben. Somehow this is all his fault, and he's nowhere to be found. Why did I agree to let him come over?" Jackson's anxiety was ratcheting up.

A few minutes later, he was trekking back along the shoreline, heading west toward the setting sun. He pointed himself at the red-orange orb as it sank in the west, leaving a thick line of burnt orange along the edge of the ever-deepening blue-black of the sky. As all color left the sky, Jackson was nearing the place where he'd fallen hard on the rocks and been confronted by the woman and her dog. He came out of his self-imposed trance at that moment, realizing he should head back to his cabin.

"Why didn't I tell the cops that Ben *stole* my boat? That I was knocked unconscious by Ben or someone else?" His head was spinning when he suddenly heard the fallen leaves being forcefully disturbed by someone going up the hill above him.

Norah could be startled by the forest's inhabitants, but she wasn't afraid of them. Humans, on the other hand? Her body taut, she raised the shovel ready to strike, but only if the intruder was human.

She heard the ever-present rocks moving under a heavy foot across the uneven surface at the edge of the woods. Then quiet swishing in the native grasses. The moon came out from behind some passing clouds long enough for her to see but not be seen. Her hands tensed on the shovel.

A man in dark clothing threw one leg over the deck's railing. Before he could get both feet on the concrete, she stepped forward and hit him squarely in the chest and face with the heavy shovel.

He grunted and toppled backward over the railing, hitting his head on the hard ground. She pulled a flashlight off her shelf and shined it in his face. It was not the face she had expected to see.

The man on the ground wasn't moving, but Norah was taking no chances. She hurried to the sliding door closest to the end of the deck and let Velma out. Velma, clearing the railing over the closed gate, emitted a threatening rumbling from her throat as she positioned herself within inches of the man's face. He didn't move. Velma, her growling increasing, bristled and stepped back. Someone was running, stumbling up their path.

Norah cast her light toward the spot at the top of the cliff where her path ended. The man emerging caught the light full in the face and stopped.

"Hey, it's, I'm your neighbor. Don't shoot!"

"What are you doing here? Are you with this guy?" Norah standing above him on the deck redirected her light down onto the man on the ground where Velma stood, shifting her position slightly so as to keep her eyes on both suspects.

"What guy? Oh, shit. Did you do that?" Jackson took a few steps toward the prone figure, but Norah's raised shovel stopped his progress. "Can I please come over there?"

Norah walked through the gate and stepped down next to Velma above the body of the unconscious man.

"Yes, slowly." She shone the light on the ground in front of him so he could see where to walk.

Jackson looked from the shovel still in Norah's hands to the bloodied face of the man on the ground. "Oh, shit. It's Ben, my fr—, this guy I used to work with." Jackson stared down at the man sprawled on the ground, the dog keeping her eyes on both men.

"I'm calling the police right now." Norah pulled her phone from her pocket.

Jackson listened to her talk to the police while he stood near Ben's still form. The woman didn't say anything to the police about Jackson showing up at her house. Only that a man had tried to get onto her deck so she hit him with her shovel.

The sirens and Velma started to howl. Norah silenced her. "Here they come. Stay, Velma. And you, you're a witness to my assault on this guy."

"Yeah, right."

"This guy, Ben, was at my house and then disappeared after stealing my boat." Jackson pointed to the man lying on the ground.

"Your friend, is he? Nevermind, the cops are at the door. Velma. Guard."

Less than a minute later, a light on the corner of the house flooded the top of the cliff with bright light. At the same time, four cops ran around the corner of the house with Norah close behind. Velma whirled around to confront them, and the cops nearly fell over each other, even though they had been warned she was there.

One officer walked over to the prone figure and bent down to check for a pulse. As he did, Ben started cursing and flaying until two other officers pinioned his arms behind him and stood him up, bloodied face to the light.

"Well, who do we have here?" One cop asked.

Another started reading the struggling man his rights, charging him with breaking and entering. "That's for stepping over this woman's railing without invitation. That's just for starters. You must be involved in whatever caused that bloody scene down the hill."

Ben began to protest his innocence as he was being hauled away by the two cops holding him on either side.

Jackson spoke for the first time, "That's Ben Sanderson." But as he spoke, the two remaining cops stepped up beside him.

"You know him, yeah? So he's your buddy who owns the car we took from your place yesterday? What are you doing *here* anyway?"

Avoiding the first questions, Jackson said, "Being taken in and grilled at your station, sorta upset me, you know? You told me not to leave, but I thought some fresh air within range of my house would be okay. As I was heading back toward my place, I heard someone in the trees going up toward her house and then the thwack and grunt when she tattooed him with her shovel. I ran up the path. She shined her flashlight in my face, called you. You know the rest."

"I can verify the last part of that statement, officer. Do you need me to come in and make a full statement now?" Norah walked up to them as she spoke. Velma beside her eyeing the three men.

"No, you can come in the morning, Ms., Mrs.?"

"Norah Brooks. Thank you. I'll be in first thing."

"Mr. Beckwith, is it? We need to ask you some questions about you and your friend, under caution." One cop took hold of Jackson's arm and steered him away around the corner.

The remaining cop turned to Norah, "That's quite a swing you have there." He smiled and walked away giving Velma a wide berth.

"Looks like our new neighbor is in for another long night or maybe worse," Norah speculated as she scratched Velma's head.

As they walked back around the house, the chill wind whirled the dead leaves around their feet.

Our Daily Bread

During their last year at university, Dahlia and her friends 'discovered' a little town not far from their university city. Strewn along the town's charming tree-lined main street were hip little shops nestled into brick buildings dating from the mid-nineteenth century. On at least one wall of every other building a mural captured some part of the town's history. These classic buildings offered more than a business venture. They were mixed-use properties, having commercial and residential spaces.

The shops at street level included second-floor rooms which many owners had converted into apartments for themselves. But, as a couple of her college friends learned to their advantage, the owners sometimes lived elsewhere and rented the apartments above their shops. The town, Drumwell, became a place where Dahlia and her friends could escape the constant buzz of university life in a short drive down a couple of pleasant, two-lane, rural highways.

A few years later, Dahlia drove into Drumwell on her own to visit a favorite coffee and tea shop. When she arrived, she ordered her hot tea and sat down undisturbed at a counter, relaxing into a view of the sunny main street of the town. As she stared out the window in front of her, she noticed a For Lease sign on the door of an empty shop across the street. Dahlia idled her meandering thoughts, finished her tea, and went across to look more closely at the sign.

As she read the description of the vacant property, Dahlia's reflections turned to memories of her mother.

Dahlia's mother had baked bread every week of her daughter's childhood, Dahlia literally learning at her mother's knee. Whenever bread-making day came around, her mother would place a small bowl on the counter in front of her child. Standing on a step stool, little Dahlia hovered over the bowl, pulling random ingredients from the various bins in a small cupboard within her reach. As the child stirred her ingredients together in her little bowl, she would pooch out her lips in deep concentration. A serious baker. By the time she was twelve, Dahlia was strong enough to stir proper ingredients together to form the bread dough—twisting, turning, and slapping the mass it made to get the yeast riled up enough for the dough to rise. At least that's what her mother always claimed was happening.

Dahlia took over the weekly bread making shortly after her fifteenth birthday, her mother becoming ill that year and too weak for stirring and kneading the dough. Three years later, the day before her mother died, Dahlia made a loaf of brown bread, from a recipe handed down for three generations. Dahlia and her mother and father had eaten the bread together, happy for the last time. In losing her mother, Dahlia also lost her desire to make bread. Her father, lost in his own grief, threw himself into his work.

Dahlia started college the Fall after her mother died. Following a bumpy first year, she managed to finish her degree in four years with a double major in history and literature. But graduation day turned into a day of mourning after a drunk driver deprived her of her father. His partner, Stan Webster, investigated the accident, above and beyond the call of duty. He was Dahlia's godfather and her father's best friend, after all.

Consequently, at 23, Dahlia was a bereaved orphan. In spite of her sorrow at having lost both parents in such a short span of time, it wasn't in Dahlia's nature to be self-indulgent or self-pitying. She came from a long line of strong women and so she put the small bequest her father left her into the bank and found a job.

Although it was the first job that had come along, it was also one she was at once hesitant and eager to undertake, apprentice baker at Frida's Daily Bread, a good-sized bakery Dahlia and her friends had frequented during their college years. She wondered if it would reignite her passion for her mother's gift of breadmaking.

Five years later, Dahlia came out of her reverie in front of the For Lease sign in downtown Drumwell and put the contact information into her phone. Within two months, Dahlia had quit her job at Frida's and leased the mixed-use property, a shop-apartment combo, on the charming, tree-lined main street of Drumwell.

Both the shop and apartment had been well-cared for by the last tenants. The shop space at street level had two outer doors, one opening onto the main street and one onto the alley in back. An inner door closed off a stairway, at the top of which was another door to the apartment on the second floor. The apartment boasted a kitchen, living room, bathroom, and a loft-style bedroom a few steps above the living room. In the loft, a window opened onto a wrought-iron landing with a gate to a fire escape. The landing was just large enough for one or two people to stand on before stepping through the gate and descending the fire escape along the outside wall down to the alley. Dahlia was a bit dubious about having window access to the fire escape in her bedroom, but her cat, Ziggy, would dig the view.

The agent that leased the place to Dahlia told her that in the '60s, it had been a head shop, selling faux-fur jackets, tie-dye clothes, smoking paraphernalia, and other choice items of the time. Its last iteration was as a homemade beeswax candle store with appropriate accoutrements.

Dahlia thought this shop-apartment combo the perfect space for a small bakery at street level with her own apartment above.

A sign, made for her by an artist friend of her mother's, would hang above the counter displaying her mother's dictum—*Kinship comes from blood and bone but also from bread and beans. Pass it on.* Dahlia would introduce bean soups and stews by winter, but the first bread would be the brown bread, the last bread she had made for her mother.

When she was emptying and stowing the items out of a box marked KITCHEN, she located the small wooden chest in which her mother always kept her recipe cards. Dahlia had been updating the family recipes with organic ingredients and her own innovations during the last year or so that she worked at Frida's. Now, she set the chest on her kitchen counter and pulled the brown bread recipe card with her own whole berry cranberry sauce recipe on the back.

"O.K.," she breathed into the room, "Let's make brown bread and cranberry sauce."

Dahlia set the card on her mother's silver recipe card stand and began taking ingredients from the cupboard and freezer, where she kept her stash of cranberries. She'd carried most of the basics from her old apartment, including the cranberries. Her mother once told her that if you want cranberries all year long, you must buy extras and freeze them. So between Thanksgiving and Christmas, when cranberries were abundant in the stores, Dahlia stocked up.

She finished making the cranberry sauce with fifteen minutes to spare before the bread was ready to slice. The sweet and sour aroma of the steaming cranberries mixing with the heady scent of the brown bread reaffirmed Dahlia's belief in her new venture.

After brewing a small pot of black tea, she carried teapot and cup to the table. Ziggy jumped down from the windowsill where he was inspecting the new sights along the main street and repositioned himself for a taste of the bread. No cranberries, please.

Sitting at the table near the same window, Dahlia sipped her tea and spread a spoonful of the warm cranberry sauce onto a slice of bread. Twenty minutes later, she leaned back against the solid oak slats of her chair and reached out to pet Ziggy's head.

"Ziggy, you probably don't remember *your* mother. She was a lovely cocoa brown with dark stripes and a perfect M on her forehead. She carried herself with great dignity and took good care of you and me. Her name was Zenobia." Dahlia grinned at her cat.

Ziggy lifted his eyes from his crumble of brown bread. He didn't have anything to say about his mother or her weird name so he went back to licking the crumbs.

Now that the apartment and Ziggy were mostly settled, Dahlia could turn her full attention to getting the bakery ready. She planned her grand opening for the first week of the university's Fall term. She still needed to hire three employees—one full-time baker, one baker's apprentice, and one part-time bakery assistant. Interviews for these positions would begin in two days.

The last of the appliances will arrive tomorrow, she realized, as she carried her cup and plate to the sink, rinsed the dishes out, and placed them in the under-the-counter dishwasher. Then Dahlia started toward the door that opened onto the stairway to the shop, Ziggy close behind.

"No, Zig. You can't come into the bakery. If it were a bookstore, absolutely, all yours. But a bakery is off limits to non-human critters. I'm sorry."

Ziggy flipped his tail to show his displeasure. When Dahlia walked through the door to head down the stairs to the shop, the cat ran into the living room and up the steps to the bedroom loft where he climbed to the top of his tall cat tree and turned his back to the doorway. When Dahlia returned, she would see for herself his disapproval, and realize her neglect.

"What was that?" Dahlia stopped to listen before crossing the threshold into the shop. The scraping, scratching sound she thought she'd heard came again. "It almost sounds like claws." Dahlia frowned as she walked toward the back door of the shop, moving quietly forward before peering out the peephole in the door.

A raccoon, looking rather the worse for wear, clawed at the garbage can. Dahlia let out a breath and walked outside, keeping a reasonable distance between her body and that of the ratty-looking raccoon.

"Shoo, you. Go on, shoo," she waved her hand as she remonstrated with the raccoon. "Leave my trash where it is!"

Dahlia knew the raccoon would merely run off out of sight until he or she was certain that the annoying human had gone. But it was strange for a raccoon to be running about downtown in daylight.

"I didn't know raccoons even came near the main street," her voice echoing in the empty shop as she closed the door behind her. She was relieved the noise was only a raccoon and guilty that human incursion had driven raccoons and other wildlife from their natural habitats into the towns.

Dahlia was puzzling over how to humanely thwart the raccoon pilfering the garbage when wind chimes started tinkling. Reaching in her pocket, she pulled out her cell phone and answered without looking at the ID.

"Hello, uh, Our Daily Bread, hello?" she stuttered.

"Dolly, hi. Is that the name of your new bakery?"

"Oh, Steven. Maybe." Don't call me Dolly. She gritted her teeth. And how did you know about my bakery?

"Well, I thought you'd want to know that I'll be in town tomorrow interviewing the new mayor."

So what. "Oh, that's nice." Who cares? "I'm sorry we won't be able to get together." Not. "My appliances for the bakery are coming tomorrow. I have to be here all day and evening," she lied about the evening while planning to make it true.

"Surely, you have to eat dinner?"

"Well, I'll just eat as I work."

"Maybe I'll stop by anyway. See you." And he clicked off.

Damn, she thought. That's all I need is Steven showing up while I'm trying to focus on getting the bakery up and running. The "Closed" shade is on the door, and I'll be sure to lock up as soon as the delivery has been made. Surely, I can keep a low profile.

Somehow Steven Burroughs had a knack for getting under her skin. For disrupting her sangfroid, her composure. After he graduated from the university, he became a local success as a journalist and moved quickly from a newspaper in town to a regional television news network. His extreme good looks hadn't hurt his transition from print to television. Nor had his matchless ego. Dahlia was certain if she saw him, she would suffer for it in some way, even though she was the one who broke off their relationship during Spring term of her senior year at the university.

Young and still naïve, Dahlia had fallen instantly for the handsome, self-confident young man she'd met at a friend's BBQ the summer after her freshman year. Steven was two years older and "heading for big things," as he claimed on their first meeting. She was too inexperienced to hear the arrogance in his declaration and he was a master at making such statements sound playful rather than cocky. But cocky he was, and when Dahlia caught him cocking it up with an intern at his first newspaper office two years later, she canned him from her life.

Unfazed, Steven Burroughs became the pesky-mosquito-ex, buzzing in and out of Dahlia's life, trying to suck her lifeblood. Sadly, citronella didn't work on human bloodsuckers. He even came to her father's funeral, giving his best performance as the spurned-but-still-concerned lover.

She turned her frustration into cleaning every surface in the public area of the bakery. Six hours later, countertop, shelves, tables, ceramic cups and saucers, espresso machine, the lot, were shining. Dahlia accepted the fact that she would probably have to clean it all again before the opening, but seeing it all sparkle at that moment made the bakery real. She turned out the lights before heading back up to her apartment.

Ziggy had given up his mythic, turn-to-you-my-back stance on the cat tree for an anguished-distraught pose next to his food bowl. Starving. Inexcusable.

"Sorry, Zig. I lost track of time. Your bowl *was* full when I went downstairs, you know." She ruffled his indignant head, reached into the cabinet for his food bin, and refilled his bowl of crunchies.

Dahlia opened her refrigerator to see if she could find something for herself. She had been so focused on getting moved and settled that, except for the cranberries in the freezer, only bare essentials and a couple of restaurant leftover boxes sat in her fridge.

"This will do!" she cried. "Leftover hummus and tabouleh from yesterday's lunch. And pita, too."

After her light repast, Dahlia felt content and extremely tired. She cleaned up her dishes, then went into her bathroom for nightly ablutions. Face washed, teeth brushed, pj's on, she stepped up to the loft and crawled into bed while Ziggy climbed his tall tree once more to stand watch over the alley. To sleep the remorseless sleep of cats.

3AM.

As a clanging sound exploded from somewhere in the alley behind the shop, Ziggy went flying down the loft steps to the living room.

Dahlia jerked awake. "What the hell was that, Zig?" She jumped up rushing down the stairs to the shop, closing both stairway doors securely behind her, leaving Ziggy safe but seething inside the apartment.

Her phone in one hand, she swiped up to turn on the flashlight. Quickly pressing the lit phone to her side, Dahlia crept forward through the shop toward the back door. Another sound rang out, like someone throwing a tin can down the street.

"That bloody raccoon is back. Must've gotten the lid off the trash can this time," she couldn't help voicing her exasperation aloud.

She hurried on to the back door. Out of habit, she peeked through the tiny opening that gave a wide angle view from the door to the edge of the parking lot across the alley. The streetlight actually worked and shed sufficient light for a visual of the whole area. Dahlia abruptly pulled her eye back from the peephole.

A man in a faded, flannel shirt and baggy pants stood with his back to her as he dug through her trash can, tossing whatever he didn't want. Dahlia wasn't sure what to do.

Deciding he must be homeless, Dahlia watched him to make sure he didn't injure himself. Compassion and care had been her parents' philosophy and practice. They taught Dahlia well. Sighing heavily, she continued to look on a bit longer, unsure if she could do more to help in the middle of the night.

In the morning, she'd call the local shelter to see what she might do to aid their efforts for the homeless in her new town. Then, she planned to call the waste disposal people again about the dumpster they promised to deliver. If he or any other homeless person came again, there'd be less chance of injury with a larger, heavy-lidded container, she thought. Or would that be worse? *At any rate, this will soon be a full-fledged business, and I'm required to have a large dumpster in place.*

Back upstairs in her apartment, Dahlia grabbed a glass of water and walked up the steps to her loft. Ziggy was, of course, livid, having been prevented from following her into the shop to see about the latest ruckus. He noisily clawed himself up his cat tree, refusing to join her on her bed for what remained of the night.

In the morning, after more brown bread, cranberries, and tea for herself and a full bowl of crunchies topped with a salmon treat for Ziggy, Dahlia a pulled on a pair of gardening gloves to go out and clean up the mess she knew would be waiting behind the shop. The clean-up took only about twenty minutes.

"That wasn't as bad as I expected, Zig," she said as she came back into the apartment. "The appliances are due by ten o'clock, so we still have plenty of time to get ready."

For the next two hours, Dahlia steam-cleaned the bakery kitchen floor for the second or third time, and made sure that nothing was in the way of the delivery people. The commercial gas stove, the baking oven, double door refrigerator, and tall proofing cabinets would easily fit in the spaces she had cleared for them. Her mixers and cooling racks were already in place.

By late afternoon, all kitchen appliances were installed. She re-steamed the floor and preparation counter, of course. Dirty work boots smeared the floor and greasy fingerprints mottled the counter.

Dahlia felt sweaty, dirty, and fabulously accomplished when she finally finished around six o'clock. She was heading upstairs to her apartment when a knock came at the front door of the shop.

A delivery person would use the door buzzer, she thought as she turned to look toward the front of the shop, so who—No. No way. Why is it you, Steven? I don't want to see you now, or ever. I am not letting you into my world again!

A bead of sweat rolled down from her hair as she shuffled along with her back to the wall, staying out of view from the front door until she reached the stairway to her apartment. Ziggy was tapping his foot for his supper when she walked in.

When Dahlia emerged from the shower, scents of lavender and coconut filled the upper floor. After she donned jeans, t-shirt, and sandals, she checked her phone. Three missed calls. All from Steven. Ignoring the waiting messages, she tucked the phone in the back pocket of her jeans and stepped down into the living room.

Now that she was clean and refreshed, she realized she was also incredibly hungry. In the kitchen, she found only one more leftover box. Two days old and skimpy.

Maybe I'll have more bread and cranberry sauce, she considered, but immediately knew that wouldn't do the trick.

"Well, Zig. I'll have to walk down to the new microbrewery at the end of the block. Good fish and chips, I've heard." She ruffled his head. He remained aloof until she gave him two more salmon treats and refilled his water and food bowls.

Outside, the air was still heavy with August heat and humidity, but she remembered reading about an outdoor patio area at the microbrewery that boasted overhead fans. She spotted the space as soon as she was halfway down the block. Every table taken. Dahlia almost turned back, but hunger propelled her forward and into the restaurant.

She was beginning to relax after her narrow escape from her ex at her place until she walked further into the restaurant. There was Steven chatting up some woman at the bar. Dahlia wanted to walk out again but was already following the hostess to a table. Feeling that an abrupt departure by a customer would be the height of rudeness and could hurt her own business down the line, she walked on. Taking the menu from the hostess, Dahlia sat down, smiling almost convincingly at the hostess.

Okay, she considered, my back *is* to the bar so Steven won't see my face. That should keep me safe.

But Steven was an expert at chatting up one woman while scanning the area for better prospects. Dahlia had immediately drawn his eye as she was being seated. One minute later, he was at her table.

"Dahlia, I thought you were busy with your new gadgets tonight, but I guess you got my message that I'd be here." Steven could smile-smirk and demean at the same time.

"Steven. Yes, well, I finished earlier than I expected." And I didn't check my messages nor expect to see you still in town. Thought you'd be scouting the talent at the university bars forty miles away by now.

"I came by your place," he whined.

"I was probably in the back alley or in the shower."

"You do smell enticing. What's that fragrance?"

Eau de Leave-Me-the-Hell-Alone. "Clean."

"You're so funny, Dahlia. Shall we order?"

A brief struggle between her desire to get away from him and her hunger, hunger won. "Sure."

She looked down at her menu and saw the fish and chips on special. That would mean fast. As usual, Steven's presence at the table beckoned a waitress like a silent whistle for a dog.

"What can I get y'all, tonight?" Lots of really white teeth shone, at Steven.

Apparently "y'all" has a different meaning at this place, Dahlia thought.

After Steven ordered, the waitress turned, sans toothy smile, to Dahlia, "And you?"

"Fish and chips and a small lemonade, please."

Another flashing smile for Steven before the waitress could find no more reason to linger. "I'll get those drinks." Flash.

Dahlia continued to study the menu as if it were a sacred document. Some interesting bread items did catch her attention. But Steven was still talking.

"And so, Dahlia, when do you plan to open? Having a big grand opening ceremony?"

"It's just a small bakery, Steven. We might have a banner across the door. Nothing elaborate."

"I'd like to be here for you that day. When is it?"

Seriously? "Not for a few weeks yet. Maybe late September," she lied.

Lying to Steven had become second nature and a necessity over the years.

"Well, let me know, and I'll be here. Unless, of course, I have a big assignment somewhere. My interview from today will be on the eleven o'clock news tonight, you know. And that's small potatoes for what's in the works."

He winked, and Dahlia thought of the Monty Python routine — 'Wink, wink, nudge, nudge, say no more.' But Steven would say more and, besides, never understood Python humor. What a dull boy, she realized. How could I have wasted two years on this guy?

As if he could hear her thoughts, Steven began reminiscing about their time together. Remember this, remember that, he quizzed. She only remembered that he couldn't keep his eyes and, ultimately, his hands off other women. Unforgivable.

The arrival of their food gave Dahlia an excuse to avoid conversation. Steven enjoyed hearing himself talk anyway, so she needn't respond while she ate. When she finished, she pulled a little leftover container from her bag for the last piece of fish and some chips.

"Well, nice to see you, Steven. I have to get to bed early. Loads to do this week. Bye." Dahlia nearly flew across the restaurant and out the door, Steven saying something as she went. She didn't know what. Cared less.

Home again and in her pj's once more, she and Ziggy curled up on the sofa and watched a cooking show until both of their heads were nodding. They barely made it up the steps to the loft and their beds.

Over her bowl of muesli and yogurt in the morning, Dahlia read the booklets for all her new appliances, though she knew them all well enough from working at Frida's. Then she began to prepare the interview sheet for the applicant interviews scheduled for tomorrow morning at five.

The first test, she thought. Anyone I hire will have to be able to be up and at work well before five o'clock. How alert are you in the wee hours? Can you be friendly to customers at 7AM after working for three or four hours? Are you conversant with the operations of a bakery? With the equipment, etc.? She finished her interview sheet and started on her supply list for the bakery, with a shorter list for the gaps in her own kitchen.

On a chalkboard affixed to her kitchen wall, she had been writing the names of breads she wanted to make as standard fare for her bakery. So far, the list included her brown bread, Irish soda bread, cornbread (traditional and spicy), cinnamon bread, and, on Sunday mornings, cinnamon rolls, biscuits, and raised doughnuts. She wrote down a few more items to the bakery supply list before patting Ziggy on the head and grabbing her bags.

"I'm off to the store now, Ziggy. You have fresh water and food, so be good." He seriously disliked being patted like a dog.

Around noon the next day, Dahlia pushed back from one of the tables in the cafe area of the bakery where she had been conducting the interviews.

Those went pretty well, she thought. It really helped to place ads around campus. But, I think I already know who I'm going to hire.

She gathered up the applications, her notes, and her empty tea cup before heading up to the apartment.

Back upstairs and seated at her walnut spinet desk in the living room, she reread the applications and her own notes for the three people she had in mind. On a blank sheet in her notebook, she wrote the position title and some brief info about each intended hire.

From a week before Thanksgiving, the bakery had been hopping. When the last special order was picked up on Wednesday at 3:00, all the staff, including Dahlia, cleaned up furiously for an hour. Then Dahlia gathered her three employees together in the small living room of her apartment.

Shed of aprons, head coverings, and flour dust, they stood with champagne glasses in hand as Dahlia offered an exuberant toast, "To all of you, without whom, this gorgeous success of ours, would not have been possible. Cheers!"

They sipped their chilled champagne, feeling exhausted but delighted.

James lifted his glass, "To Dahlia Clarke, brilliant baker and boss extraordinaire!"

"Hear, hear," agreed Mindy and Callie.

Dahlia grinned broadly, regarding the little group as they sipped more champagne and began to sample the hors d'oeuvres she had made the night before, finishing about four hours before her alarm went off.

"Thank you all for staying to the glorious end of this, our first holiday triumph. Here's to a pleasant short break tomorrow and Friday before—who's coming to help me on Saturday morning?" Dahlia's eyes considered each one in turn.

"I am, chef. No family to worry about so I'll be available whatever time you need me to come." James grinned.

"Oh, I thought you'd be heading back to the Bay Area to visit friends. Truth be told, you all, I could handle Saturday on my own."

Simultaneously, Mindy and Callie expressed their willingness to forego their family gatherings, if need be. Then went back to petting and whispering endearments to Ziggy, who smirked from the arm of the sofa.

James shifted his weight, "I'm not leaving town. Friends are all scattered now. I'll just sleep in and be ready to come in Saturday, whatever time you say."

"If you're sure, James, that would be great. But . . . since you're in town on your own, you should come over tomorrow for Thanksgiving with Ziggy and me and a couple of my friends. It'll be a Cajun-style Thanksgiving. Jasmine is making her famous shrimp and grits, and Florent, Jas's husband has promised a variety of treats for dessert. I'm making cornbread with a kick and maque choux. You could bring any dish you want.

"I'd love to come. What time?"

"Sleep in. We'll start celebrating about two o'clock. Dinner at three."

The other two had shifted their attention from Ziggy to the snacks while Dahlia poured the last of the champagne into each glass.

"To us and Our Daily Bread," all shouted, lifting their glasses one more time.

CLANG.

Dahlia woke with a start.

"Ziggy, wha—" but the words died in her mouth as she saw, backlit by the weak streetlight, the side of a pale, white face pressed against the window pane, one eye leering, searching.

Suddenly, Ziggy flew off his tall tree screeching and clawing at the glass. The eye disappeared instantly, and the clanging repeated in double time down the fire escape. Then, silence.

"Ziggy, baby, you saved us. But from who or what I'm not sure." Dahlia exclaimed, dialing 9-1-1 as she did.

When two police officers arrived at her shop door ten minutes later, she was dressed and waiting. She showed them in, the bakery now well-lit. As she described what happened, she walked them up the inner stairway into her apartment. Ziggy was on the table glaring and growling.

The two officers gave him a wide berth as they followed Dahlia to the loft window. One climbed through the window and the other told Dahlia to shut the window behind his partner and lock it. He would go down and meet the other officer in the alley below. At the back door of the shop, the policeman stepped out with Dahlia behind him. He motioned her to stay close to the door.

The two cops stood at the base of the winding fire escape talking. Then they walked slowly back toward Dahlia.

"Ma'am, it's impossible to tell who or what might have been on that stairway. Are you sure you weren't dreaming?"

Prick. "Of course not. I saw his pale, white skin and one eye and heard the clanging as he ran down each step after clearing the little gate at the top. My cat attacked the glass and scared the shit out of whoever was peering in." Dahlia refused to be labeled an hysterical woman.

"O.K., we'll search the alleyway but can't promise the guy isn't long gone. I doubt if we'll find any evidence either." The second cop, toned it down but oozed skepticism.

She thanked them (for what, she wasn't sure) and went back inside, turning off lights as she went. In her own little kitchen, she was sure of one thing. She wouldn't be sleeping any more tonight.

"It's 4 AM, Thanksgiving morning, Ziggy."

The cat jumped off the table and headed for his food bowl. Apparently, being ferocious and brave made him hungry.

"Good idea, Zig." Dahlia gave the cat his breakfast and then pulled the brown bread and cranberries from the fridge.

She put the kettle on for tea and put a spoonful of sugar in her cup. Between shock at the peeper and anger at the attitude of the cops, her body was still vibrating. She sipped her tea, and gradually the tension and anger eased. Dahlia tried to think about her Thanksgiving dinner party.

"Did I remember the jalapeños? Yesterday's grocery run feels like a distant dream," she confided in Ziggy as she pulled the cornbread recipe from the wooden chest and gathered the ingredients.

A few hours later, she was nearly ready for her guests as she put the cornbread in the oven.

"By the time the bread is done, I'll be clean and fresh for you, hon," she sang out in an old-style bluesy beat.

By 1:45, the house and Dahlia were ready for guests. She expanded and elevated her Italian-made maple wood table to set places for four with a woven cornucopia in the center of the table, small Granny Smith apples, Bosc pears, and popcorn balls spilling out the open end.

The door buzzer at the front of the shop went off. Leaving Ziggy fuming once again in the apartment, Dahlia ran down the stairway and across the floor of the shop to the front door.

"Jasmine, Florent. It's so good to see you all!" Dahlia cried and hugged each friend in turn.

"You, too, my friend. Not visiting the fam this year since Florent's mad uncle will be there. I couldn't take any more of his see-I'm-not-a-racist humor." Jasmine rolled her eyes.

As Dahlia started to close the door, James arrived with a small, painted wooden case in one hand and a covered bowl in the other.

He held up the bowl. "Spicy cabbage slaw with jalapeños, red bell pepper, green onions, lime juice, and a bit more. Not strictly Cajun, but it should complement the dishes you mentioned." James handed Dahlia the wooden case. Inside, she found two bottles of wine—one pinot noir and one sauvignon blanc. "The case is for you. To keep." Neither James nor Dahlia noticed Jasmine's raised eyebrows nor her elbow poking Florent's oblivious side.

"Sounds great," Florent said, wincing.

"Thank you so much, James."

Dahlia introduced him to her friends, and greetings were exchanged as the four made their way with the various foodstuffs up to Dahlia's apartment.

"Dahlia, I love your table," Jasmine crooned. *Laissez les bon temps rouler!*"

"Yes, let the good times roll!" Dahlia laughed as she went to the kitchen to get the bottle of Prosecco that had been chilling overnight.

After dinner, Jasmine and Dahlia were in the kitchen choosing another wine and catching up, Jasmine regaling Dahlia with the activities of her colleagues at the law firm.

"They are seriously deranged but relieve a lot of tension that comes with every new case and with those seemingly never-ending ones."

"Good colleagues make all the difference," Dahlia agreed.

"Speaking of which, how are *your* new colleagues," Jasmine tilted her head toward the living room where Florent and James were searching through Dahlia's CD collection for more music.

"They're great, all of them." Noncommittal.

"And?"

"And I'm very happy with their work and attitudes."

"And?"

"Jas, well, I—James is an amazing baker. And I'm *not* blind." Dahlia pressed her lips together as if to keep from saying more.

Jasmine noticed, "Well, any sparks? If not for lovin' Florent, I'd be sparkin'."

Dahlia laughed. "I know you would, but I don't want to complicate the amazing dynamics among the four of us in the bakery."

At that moment, Ziggy strolled into the kitchen to see if a tidbit might be in the offing when he abruptly stopped moving. His tail bushed out. At the same time, all his fur stood up on end, a growl emanating from deep within.

"Ziggy? What's the matter, baby?" Dahlia frowned and started to walk over to him when she heard a metallic clanging, echoing, dying out.

"Dahlia, what's going on?" Jasmine's face had gone from impish to alarmed.

"I don't know. May be connected to that window peeper last night."

"What! You didn't tell us about any window creeps. Damn, girl. Tell." Jasmine, hands on hips, was not to be denied.

"First, I need to go up to the loft window that leads to the fire escape."

"Not alone, you're not. Florent! James." Jasmine started to shout then lowered the volume.

The two men hurried into the kitchen glancing all round the room as they did.

"Jassy, what is it, baby?" Florent crooned.

"Not me, Florent. Dahlia has something to tell us while *we all*" emphasis added, "check out that noise."

"What noise?" Florent again.

"I thought it was in the alley, Dahlia. Holiday drunks or those raccoons?" James read Dahlia's expression and frowned. "What do *you* think it is?"

"I had a peeping Tom last night. He might be back. Follow me. Quietly." Dahlia's stage whisper, commanding, as she walked out of the kitchen and into the living room.

They formed a line behind her matching her silence and her pace as she went across the living room toward the steps to the loft. She stopped.

"That window, about a quarter of the way along the wall," she pointed up toward the right side of the loft, "opens onto a small landing with a gate to the fire escape leading down to the alley behind the shop. I need to see if anyone is out there."

"Let me do it, Dahlia. Your peeper wouldn't expect me." James offered.

"All right, but let me get hold of Ziggy. He attacked the face at the window last night."

Dahlia picked up the cat and motioned to Florent and Jasmine to move to the other side of the room with her. They did without comment.

James moved slowly up the steps to the loft and then sat with his back to the wall, pushing himself along with his hands toward the window. When he reached it, he slowly craned his neck so his eyes were in a position to see out without his immediately being seen. When he stretched his whole body to stand up against the wall, Dahlia's breath caught.

"No one's out there," he said, turning toward the room.

"Then I need to go to the back door of the shop. I have a wide angle viewer in the door so I can see all of the back area including the alley directly behind it." Dahlia set Ziggy down on a chair and headed for the door and stairway to the shop.

"We're all going," Jasmine said firmly.

They lined up again, the last one, Jasmine, making sure the door was shut with Ziggy inside the apartment.

The second stairway door opened onto a hallway where there was an all-gender toilet for the customers and, at the end, the back door. Dahlia went right to the peephole while the others gathered behind her."What do you see," Florent asked, keeping his voice low.

"Nothing." Clipped. Puzzled.

"Maybe James was right. Just holiday revelers stumbling down the alley." Florent optimistic.

Dahlia shook her head, "No. The sound, the clanging. Must have been the dumpster lid. I'm going out there."

"Not alone," they chorused.

The four friends poured out the back door, Dahlia having turned her floodlight on before they went.

James was first into the alley, Florent close behind. Florent said something to James, and they walked in opposite directions. James went north a half block to the next street while Florent walked down another half block to the south before turning back to meet James behind Dahlia's car.

Before either could speak, Dahlia did, "Just like when the cops came and found no trace of anyone or any disturbance." She frowned, fully frustrated.

Then she saw a single shoe on the ground next to her dumpster and bent down to get a closer look.

"Raccoons can't get this giant lid open and don't wear shoes! Does this belong to some drunk passerby, who stumbled against the bin, and lost his shoe?" She held up the shoe with a stick she had found nearby.

"We should call the police." Jasmine. Practical.

"They won't do diddly, so I'm tossing this shoe into the dumpster with the rest of the trash." Dahlia pushed the bin lid up and started to throw the shoe inside, but instantly stepped back letting go of the lid.

James caught it in mid descent. Florent and Jasmine stepped forward, Jasmine putting her hand out to steady Dahlia who was thrown off balance by her own sudden reaction.

"What is—" James stared, mouth agape for a second, then continued, "that? A person or a pile of old clothes?"

Dahlia peered again into the dumpster. "That's him. The old homeless man I saw digging in my trash can at the end of the summer. Same raggedy clothes." She pulled herself together and dialed 9-1-1 for the second night in a row.

Fifteen minutes later, she growled, "The police are slower tonight. Probably overstuffed like the turkeys they ate.

The four huddled together in the alley not saying much or moving until the police finally arrived. No flashing lights or siren.

Dahlia met them before they could say anything, "There's a body in my dumpster, a homeless man."

"Are you sure?" the same Skeptic as before.

"Yes, I saw him in August digging in my trash. He was wearing the same clothes. Found a shoe on the ground next to the dumpster, opened the lid to toss it in, and there he was. Is." Dahlia's patience with these condescending cops wearing thin.

When the two officers turned on their flashlights and shone the beams inside the dumpster, each took a quick step back, "Oh."

"I'll call it in," said the Skeptic.

"You need to go inside your store while we wait for the M.E. van and detectives," the other said.

Dahlia led the way back into the bakery to the cafe area where people had been enjoying her lentil soup and cornbread only yesterday.

Was it only hours and not weeks, she wondered, automatically asking her friends if they wanted coffee, tea, water, anything?

"Coffee would be nice," said the less patronizing officer who came in the door just then.

"Dahlia, please let me get it," James.

"Thank you. I—," Dahlia suddenly sat down at a table, Florent and Jasmine sliding into two of the other chairs beside her.

She was drained, incredulous at this horrible end to such a happy day and pleasant evening. Jasmine put her hand over Dahlia's cold one and flashed her concern at Florent.

Shortly, James came out of the kitchen with steaming mugs and two paper cups on a tray. He set the tray down on the table and carried the paper cups of coffee to the cop standing by the alley door.

When two detectives arrived a while later, one came over and put a hand on Dahlia's shoulder. Dahlia looked up and recognized the man who had been her dad's best friend.

"Stan, I'm so glad you're here. Can you tell us anything about why that poor homeless man might have been killed?"

"You know how it goes, Dahlia. It's too soon to say anything, and I won't be able to divulge what we learn unless you need to know." Webster shook his head, earnestly sorry for what she was going through. Then he and the other detective went back outside.

A few hours later, the detectives had asked a few preliminary questions, the M.E. van had carried the body away, and the crime scene crew had finished going over the area with their own version of the proverbial fine-toothed comb. And they had fingerprinted Dahlia and James, who touched the lid to the trash bin.

Dahlia and James now stood near the front door, Jasmine and Florent having left a few minutes before.

"Dahlia, I could stay on your sofa tonight if you don't want to be here alone," James's voice low, reassuring.

"This is my place, and I can't let anything destroy my peace. And, I don't want to put you out." Her assertion surprised him but did not dislodge his concern.

"Well, I can stay here in the shop if you'd prefer someone watching this area."

"No. I just need to lock up and put the alarm on. I keep forgetting to do that. Such a small, seemingly benign town. I'm sorry. I'm more disturbed by this than I would have imagined. My dad and Stan Webster were friends for years. I'm glad he's on this case. My dad was a homicide detective and tried, usually unsuccessfully, to prevent me from seeing the graphic nature of the crimes he and Webster worked in the city beyond what appeared in the newspapers or on television. But, he caught me snooping in his notes more than once. I didn't see any blood on that poor homeless man in the dumpster. Why him?" Dahlia turned and started for the back of the bakery.

James didn't try to answer the unanswerable question she'd asked and was resigned to let his offer to stay drop.

She checked the back door lock first and set the alarm on the wall nearby. Then walked to the front. James started to grab his coat from the chair when Dahlia turned, having just checked the lock on the front door.

"Thank you for staying, James. Let's go upstairs. I'll get you some blankets and sheets."

When they returned to Dahlia's apartment, she went into the living room, beckoning James to come with her. Dahlia walked over to an antique, wooden chest near bookshelves that met at the corner of the room. She pulled sheets, a heavy comforter, and a pillow from the chest.

"I hope you'll be comfortable on the sofa. It pulls out into a double bed." As Dahlia spoke she lifted the top of the wood table they had used earlier and began to turn and fold the table into a much smaller piece.

James thought it was a dining room table moved from another room for their meal. With a few deft moves, Dahlia had turned it into a coffee table, and only as she lifted up one end and began to roll it to one side of the room, did James see its wheels.

"That has to be the coolest table I've ever seen," he exclaimed.
"My father gave it to me for graduation a week before the ceremony. Which turned out to be a week before he died," Dahlia's tone sad but matter-of-fact.

"I'm sorry. I didn't know you had lost your dad."
"You couldn't."
James sighed, "You must be exhausted. I'll pull the bed out, if you show me how, and I'll make it up myself. Then you can go on up to bed."
James began removing the sofa cushions. As he set the last one on the converted table, Dahlia walked up to the mid-section of the sofa, reached down to a handle, previously unseen, and pulled. In one smooth motion, Dahlia now converted the sofa into a bed.
"I hope you sleep well," she smiled weakly and went into the bathroom.
A few minutes later, she came out and stepped up into the loft. As she did, she said, almost over her shoulder, "Thank you again, James. I think I can sleep now."
Soon, he was lying on the sofa bed drifting in and out of sleep. Ziggy watching him from his cat perch.

When James woke in the morning, a cat face, an inch from his nose, glared down at him.
"Good morning, kitty," James sat up and stretched his upper torso as Ziggy jumped down. Dahlia was in the kitchen so he got up and joined her.

"I think your cat and I were bunk mates last night," he laughed.

"I wondered. He usually spends half the night in my bed and half on his cat tree right by that window."

Still distressed, James wondered? A murdered man in your dumpster and a peeping Tom the night before. That's enough to unsettle any one, he thought.

"Coffee and cherry Danish?" she asked, holding out a cup.

"Did you get up and make pastries as well as hand-pressed coffee?" James was impressed.

"No. I bought the pastries Wednesday from the pastry chef I used to work with at Frida's Bakery."

"I've tried to make Danish, but they never come out light enough. These are extraordinary," he said, taking another bite of the warm cherry topping and buttery crust beneath. "How long did you work there?"

As Dahlia sat down with her coffee and pastry, she began telling James something of her story. Her mother's artistry in bronze and wood, pointing to the bronze rendering of a humpback whale and her calf sitting atop her spinet desk, and in breadmaking. The latter influenced Dahlia's decision to become a baker. Her father's death on his way to her graduation was too much. Had broken her spirit. But when she went to work at Frida's, bread making healed it. Since the window peeper and the body in her dumpster, she has felt more vulnerable than at any time in her life.

"Sorry. It's not a feeling I'm used to having. Only Jasmine knows so much about me." Dahlia shifted in her seat not looking at James.

"Nothing to be sorry about. I'm glad you felt you could share that with me." He wanted to reach out, touch her hand, tell her he understood.

"Tell me about you."

He wasn't expecting that. "It's a familiar tale in the inner city, whichever one you're from. For me, that was Sacramento. My parents were both always there for me until my dad became just another black male statistic. He was shot when I was ten."

"How awful," Dahlia's sympathetic nod encouraged him to continue.

"He was killed at the corner store picking up sugar or milk, something basic. Two thugs came in waving guns. My dad stepped between one of them and an old woman who screamed. One punk fired wildly in the direction of the scream. Sadly, he hit my dad *and* the woman Dad was trying to protect. My mother—well, I had no siblings, just my maternal grandmother and mom.

"Grandma had no sympathy for anyone but herself. When my mother went back to work, after dad was killed, I used to plead with Mom to stay home. She worked at a bank. I was so afraid that she'd be shot, too. Instead, she died of brain cancer when I was twenty. Five years later, my harping burden of a grandmother died at 93. But I have to give her credit, she stood by me through my troubles after mom died."

"What were those 'troubles'?"

"More of the usual, bored cops cruising the streets pulling over to harass a black man walking alone. One cop threw me up against their car while the other searched me. He found a couple of joints in my jacket pocket. That was probably a year before Schwarzenegger signed the bill making less than an ounce a misdemeanor. I spent the next three years in Cal State, Sacramento. Not the university, the state prison. A few months into my sentence, I was sent to work in the prison kitchen. First, I learned to cook, then bake bread. That was my salvation," James stopped, watching Dahlia's expression.

"California wasn't quite as progressive as I thought. Two joints. Damn." Dahlia sat up in her chair. "How did you get a job after you were released? I know that can be a big obstacle for anyone with a prison record."

"I was lucky. When I got out of SAC, I heard about an ex-con in Oakland who'd opened a bakery, hiring only other ex-cons. I took the next bus out of Sacramento. Less than 3 hours later, I was standing at the door of Conrad's Amazing Breads. Conrad hired me on the spot. One of his workers had quit earlier that week. I learned a lot working for him."

"How did you end up in Oklahoma? Sorry. I'm interrogating you. Must be the after effects from the cops last night."

"Not a problem. I followed a woman here where her family lived. Her mother was, well, completely crazy. She threw a major guilt trip on Cecile to get her back home. We'd been together for a year so we both quit our jobs, packed the car, and headed for Oklahoma."

"That had to be intense."

"To say the least. I won't go into the gory details, but Cecile and I lasted one month after we arrived. I looked for another bakery job, but the best I could find was a cook's job, making a bit of bread here and there. Eventually, I enrolled at OSUIT. I was about to give up on finding a job when I saw your ad."

Buzz. Dahlia stood up and walked to the door.

Stan Webster and the other detective from Stillwater.

"Come in."

"Dahlia, I'm sorry this happened to you, but we need to ask you a few more questions." His eyes roved past her and landed on James standing by the table.

"You were here last night, Mister?" the other detective now.

"Woodson. James Woodson. Yes, I was. I work here."

The two detectives asked their questions, expanding only slightly on those of the night before—did you know the victim, could you tell us any more about what caused you to go outside and look in the dumpster, could you describe your Wednesday night Peeping Tom? Dahlia and James gave them the only responses they could—didn't know the homeless man, heard the sounds, saw the shoe, the events of the night before sent us outside, only that he was white and male, maybe had brown hair.

Dahlia let Stan Webster and the other detective out of her shop, closing the door behind them. "I just hope they can actually solve this. Stan and my dad worked more than a few homicide cases together with small town police forces like this one. Not a lot of cooperation and a good bit of resentment."

Three weeks later, the winter holiday rush was on at the bakery, and every day was exhausting. But the team that Dahlia had put together worked seamlessly. Shortly before Christmas Day, Jasmine called Dahlia as she was locking up for the evening.

"Dahlia, I've got news. You can't tell anyone else yet, but I thought you should know. They caught the asshole murderer. You know, of the homeless guy in your dumpster. A major drug dealer out of Wichita who thought the homeless guy had seen him with others doing a major deal the night before. He also admitted to peeping in your window. Apparently, he thought the cat was a stray and your shop, a possible place for the drop. Anyway, I got the news through the prosecutorial grapevine. Good news! Gotta go. See you Christmas Eve."

Dahlia pulled the Closed shade down and headed for her apartment. Upstairs, she fed Ziggy and sat down at the kitchen table. At that moment, her cell phone chimed a call.

"Dahlia, this is Stan Webster. I have some good news."

After she hung up the phone, she whirled around, "Ziggy, they got him. That murdering bastard who scared us and killed that poor, homeless man is headed for a long stint in prison, maybe execution in this state."

While she sat on the sofa petting Ziggy, the shadows in the room lengthened, then disappeared into the darkness.

Dahlia's Recipes

Like most cooks and bakers, Dahlia has her own predilections. For her, organic ingredients are key. She also uses only eggs from chickens that have been pasture-raised. The quantities in each of the recipes that follow are for home kitchens.

Mama's Brown Bread, Dahlia's Way

Makes one loaf

Preheat oven to 325° and lightly oil a loaf pan or use non-stick

⅔c organic unbleached flour
⅔ c organic whole wheat flour
⅔ c organic coarse-medium grind cornmeal
1⅓ tsp baking soda
⅔ tsp organic sea salt.
1⅓ c organic whole milk yogurt
½ c organic blackstrap molasses
½ c organic walnuts, whole or pieces (optional)

Mix together dry ingredients and set aside. Measure molasses and then add to the measure of yogurt. Mix thoroughly, then pour into the dry ingredients. Stir until the batter is well-mixed. Fold in the walnuts, if using. Pour batter into prepared loaf pan.

Let bread cool in the pan for about 10 minutes (if you can wait that long). Remove from pan and slice. Best served very warm with butter or, especially good, with fresh, homemade, whole cranberry sauce. Great alongside lentil or split pea soups, too.

Whole Berry Spiced Cranberry Sauce

1 12 oz. package of organic cranberries
¼ c organic turbinado sugar
1½ c water
juice & zest from ½ large organic orange
½ tsp ground organic cinnamon
½ tsp ground organic ginger
¼ tsp. freshly grated organic nutmeg

Rinse cranberries in clear water; then place them in a medium saucepan along with the water and turbinado. Stir thoroughly and bring to a boil. Reduce the heat to simmer and add the rest of the ingredients, mixing them in completely. Cook, stirring often, until the cranberries have "popped" and the liquid is thickened, 15-20 minutes. Take the pan off the burner and let sit uncovered for 15 more minutes.

Dahlia's Cornbread with a Kick*

Makes one 9-inch round (easily doubled)

Preheat oven to 425° and lightly oil a round pan or use non-stick

    1 c organic medium grind cornmeal
    1 c organic unbleached flour
    4 tsp Rumford non-aluminum baking powder
    1 tsp organic sea salt
    1½ T organic turbinado sugar
    1½ c whole organic cow's milk or organic hemp milk
    1 pasture raised egg or egg replacement**
    2 T organic canola oil
    1 large organic jalapeño pepper, diced small

Grease and flour pan(s), and set aside.

Mix dry ingredients together. Measure milk; then add egg or egg replacement and canola oil to the milk and mix thoroughly. Add the milk, egg, and oil mixture to the dry ingredients. Stir in the diced jalapeño. Blend well. The dough should be the consistency of a thick batter.

Pour the cornbread batter into the prepared round pan. Bake for 18-20 minutes until golden on top. Pierce with a chopstick for doneness.

Place the finished bread in its pan on a cooling rack. Let rest about 5-10 minutes before removing from pan. Serve warm with butter.

*For traditional cornbread, omit jalapeños.

**For a vegan cornbread, Dahlia's personal favorite egg replacement is 1 T flax seeds + 3 T water blended with a fork until viscous. Replaces one egg.

Irish Soda Bread

Makes one loaf

Preheat oven to 375° and lightly oil a round pan or use non-stick

⅝ tsp. organic baking soda
1½ tsp. Rumford non-aluminum baking powder
⅝ tsp. organic sea salt
1 c organic unbleached flour
1 c organic whole wheat flour
1-2 T organic caraway seed
⅝ c organic, plain whole milk yogurt with ¼ c water
1 pasture-raised egg

Mix together dry ingredients (soda, baking powder, salt, unbleached flour, wheat flour and caraway seed).

Beat yogurt, water, and egg together, and add this mixture to the dry ingredients until well-mixed and balling up.

With whole wheat-floured hands, knead the dough a bit in the bowl, folding it and turning it by hand. Don't be afraid to add whole wheat flour to the dough as you add it to your hands—just don't overdo it. If it is too dry (flour density varies a good bit), carefully add a dollop of whole milk yogurt and fold that in thoroughly. Knead only until the dough is smooth and able to be formed into a spherical shape, not a ball.

Place the dough in a greased round pan and flatten it slightly with the palm of your hand. Then, score an **X** into the top, not too deeply. Bake for about 30-35 minutes.

This is best served very warm with butter and goes brilliantly with soups especially yellow split pea soup and vegetable soups. With or without the caraways, it is fabulous when toasted. Easy to double this recipe and get two loaves.

Red Lentil Soup

2 c organic red lentils

2 c water to cover dried lentils

2 c organic vegetable broth*

3-4 c boiling water

1 T organic butter or organic canola oil

10 organic baby carrots, cut in halves or thirds; or 2 large organic carrots, peeled and chopped

2 large sticks of organic celery, chopped

2 large organic parsnips, sliced in circles

1 T dried organic dill

2 tsp. organic celery seed

1 tsp. organic dried basil

1 tsp. organic dried parsley

1-2 T organic tamari

2 organic bay leaves

Soak red lentils in water in a covered bowl for 30 minutes. The amount of water is approximate. There should be enough to cover the dried lentils well with room for them to expand.

While the red lentils are soaking, melt the butter or oil in a Dutch oven on medium heat. Add the carrots, celery, and parsnips, and sauté for about 5 minutes. Mix in the dill weed, celery seed, basil, and parsley. Sauté for an additional 1-2 minutes.

Drain the red lentils, and add them to the vegetables. Immediately add the vegetable broth to the pan and stir. Add approximately 4 more cups of boiling water from the kettle.

Mix in the tamari, and add the bay leaves.** Bring to the boil; then reduce heat to simmer and cover. Simmer for about 25-30 minutes stirring occasionally. The red lentils will have turned a muted yellow, and the broth of the soup will have thickened.

Serve hot with freshly baked cornbread (which can be made, start to finish, during the simmer).

*To make vegetable broth from bouillon "paste" add 2-3 T of paste to 2 cups boiling water and stir until dissolved.

**You can leave the bay leaves in the leftover soup and discard when the last of the soup is consumed.

Mama's Basic White and/or Cinnamon Bread/Rolls ~ Dahlia's Style

Makes two loaves or a dozen rolls, or a combination thereof

Preheat oven to 350° and lightly oil loaf pans and/or flat, bread pan or use non-stick

  1 c. organic whole milk or organic hemp milk
  1 c. water
  2 tsp. organic sea salt
  4 tsp. organic turbinado sugar (or slightly less to taste)
  4 T organic butter
  4½ tsp. (2 pkgs.) dry yeast (do not use rapid rise)
  6 c. organic unbleached flour*

Scald water and milk. Do not boil. Pour warm milk-water over salt, sugar, and butter when the temp is at 110°, add yeast and mix thoroughly.

Add in flour, one cup at a time, to form a mass of dough still slightly sticky to the touch.

Place the dough in a buttered bowl and cover it with a cotton towel. Let rise about 1 to 1 ½ hours. Punch down when it has risen. Divide the dough in half** to make 2 plain loaves or a dozen or more rolls. Let rise again until double in size. Bake loaves for approximately 30 minutes. Rolls will take about half that time.

* For whole wheat divide flours in half, i.e. approximately 3 cups whole wheat and 3 cups unbleached.

**At this point, you can make cinnamon loaves and/or cinnamon rolls. For loaves, roll each half out to about ½ inch depth. Spread butter on each half (thin or thick, to taste). Sprinkle cinnamon-sugar mixture evenly onto each half (1:4 ratio, i.e. ¼ c. cinnamon to 1 c. sugar *or* 1 T cinnamon to ¼ c sugar, depending on how many loaves, rolls you are making). Roll the spiced dough lengthwise and tuck it underneath to secure, placing each tucked-side down in the loaf pans. If you want cinnamon rolls, do all the same steps, but, instead of putting in a loaf pan, cut the roll of spiced dough at ½ inch intervals, laying each slice on a flat bread tray for baking. Cinnamon rolls will take about half the baking time of loaves.

Dahlia's Biscuits

Preheat oven to 425° and lightly oil a flat bread tray or use non-stick

2 c organic unbleached flour
½ tsp organic sea salt
4 tsp Rumford non-aluminum baking powder
½ tsp organic cream of tartar
1½ T organic turbinado sugar
1 stick organic butter
⅔ c organic whole milk or organic hemp milk

Mix together all dry ingredients (flour, salt, baking powder, cream of tartar and sugar). Cut in butter with a pastry cutter or fork until the mixture is making pea-sized crumbles.

Add the milk and stir with a fork until dough ball starts to form (start with the ⅔ c and gradually add more milk as necessary to make the ball.

Place the dough onto a lightly floured surface and roll out to half-inch thickness. Cut the biscuits to the size you like and place them on a cookie sheet.

Bake for 10-13 minutes until lightly golden brown.

Mama's Yeast Doughnuts

Makes a Baker's dozen or so

Heat deep fryer to 375°

    2¼ tsp (1 pkg.) dry yeast
    1 c organic whole milk or organic hemp milk
    3 ½ c. organic unbleached flour
    ¼ c. (a half stick of butter)
    ¼ c. or less of organic turbinado sugar
    1 tsp organic sea salt
    1 pasture-raised egg
    1 quart oil for deep frying

Dissolve yeast in warmed milk (not more or less than 110°) for at least five minutes. Add 1½ c flour and beat until smooth. Cover, let stand until double (about 2 hours).

Combine butter, sugar, salt, and egg, mix well, and stir into yeast sponge. Add remaining flour and beat thoroughly. Rub with butter; let rise again until double (another 2 hours).

Roll out dough to ½ inch thick; then cut individual doughnuts with doughnut cutter. Let them rise a third time until about double (about 1 hour).

Deep fry about 3 or 4 at a time until golden brown (don't overcrowd them or oil will splash). Fry for about 1½ minutes per side. Drain on paper towels. Roll in sugar or other desired topping.

Lover Man

The fog off the bay drifted into the City and slithered around the streets. Bette couldn't see a foot in front of her. But, the neon sign protruding from the wall, signaling the jazz club, guided her.

Inside the club, she shook the late January fog-mist out of her dark, auburn hair, glowing copper in the fluorescent above the door. When her eyes adjusted to the interior low lights, she could almost see the frenetic energy of the teenage jazz fans packed in behind the wire barrier that fenced them off from the legal drinkers. The table, in the far left corner down front, sat unoccupied. Her favorite spot when she came in alone out of the dark, out of sight.

Kenny Dorham was blowing his horn, playing a tune that made her thoughtful and melancholy, "Lover Man." These cats were at the Jazz Workshop most nights but this Wednesday night, Cal Tjader stepped off so Dorham could play one tune on the triangular stage at The Black Hawk. Rumor was that Trane started playing his solo in the kitchen hallway to give Cannonball time to get off the tiny stage at her jazz club on the corner of Turk and Hyde. Hers in mind only. San Francisco and The Black Hawk were like heaven to this poor working girl in love with the ocean, jazz, and Dashiell Hammett.

She sipped her vodka gimlet as she listened to Dorham begin his jam. Later, engrossed in Tjader's "Triste," she didn't see the man walk into the club. Tiny droplets of night-mist clinging to his long wool coat, his black hair glistening under that same fluorescent. Then he slipped into the chair beside her.

"What are you doing here?" Bette snapped.

"It's a free country. What are *you* doing *here*?" His shark eyes bored through her as he spoke.

Bette shoved her chair back and stood up just as the last notes of Tjader's percussive beats faded around the room. She wasted no time in talk but, eluding the man's grasp, zigzagged like an ice skater through the crowd of tables and people. She was outside in an instant, moving along Turk street to be swallowed up by the fog.

When the man stepped out of the nightclub only a moment later, he turned his head from side to side, trying, yet failing, to see through the fog and mist. His shoulders slumped, and he shoved his hands into his coat pockets as he turned down Turk, in the opposite direction. He hailed a cab.

The fog that shielded her on Turk Street thickened, slowed her down as she walked. In a few more beats, she could make out the 288 Club's neon sign above Manuel's Steakhouse on Leavenworth. She crossed Turk onto Leavenworth for a few feet to the Page Hotel. Her one-room apartment was large, but nothing to write home about.

In fact, she'd not written to anyone about the place she now called home, except her best friend, Sandy. The day Bette arrived in the City, she sent Sandy their agreed-upon signal—one ring of the phone. That was in early December. This month, her second in San Francisco, she felt safe enough to send Sandy a long, detailed letter with her address at The Page. Only today, she received Sandy's reply assuring her that the man was clueless about Bette's whereabouts. Yet, somehow, he had found her.

In her apartment, Bette shed her coat, tossing it across the faded brocade of the overstuffed chair near the door as she pushed the button for the overhead light. The single bulb covered by a dirty, etched glass dome, barely illuminated the space. The dark corners swallowing up the light.

She plucked her cosmetics bag out of the top drawer of the old bureau before going into her tiny, private bath. The privacy strained her meagre budget some, but she couldn't imagine sharing a bathroom with the rest of the people who inhabited this floor.

When she crawled into her bed a few minutes later, the lumpy mattress, along with the shock of seeing the man tonight, kept her tossing and turning. Nothing would feel comfortable or be comforting again until she exorcised that stalking demon from her life. For good.

But how? And how had he found her here, a couple thousand miles from their hometown? She racked her brain, searching for any missteps.

Sandy had driven Bette all the way to Lawrence, Kansas so she could catch the St. Louis bus to San Francisco. Three days later just before noon, she was standing in the Greyhound Station at 425 Mission Street feeling bone tired, hungry and finally home.

The one time her parents condescended to include her in the only vacation they'd ever taken as a family, they drove West. As usual, her parents argued most of the way, while Bette concentrated hard on her Nancy Drew books.

When they reached the California coast, Bette saw the ocean and fell in love. A year later her parents split up for good, and Bette lived a nomadic life, shuffled back and forth between still-bickering parents. During those years, her recurring dream was living in California with Pacific waves crashing on a beach. In those dreams, she was blissfully alone.

When she was a teenager, she discovered jazz and bought her first jazz album, Cal Tjader, "Live at The Black Hawk." San Francisco and its jazz scene, especially The Black Hawk, infiltrated her California dream.

During high school, Bette took typing, shorthand, and secretarial training courses, to secure her independence. Senior year, she qualified for on-the-job training with the local newspaper. The editor was so impressed, he hired her full-time as soon as she graduated.

Eight years later she arrived in San Francisco with substantial work experience and fully believed she'd have no problem finding a job. But experience had to be verified by references. She couldn't give any from the one job she'd ever held. The newspaper's owner and editor was the stalker's father. No references possible. After two weeks of pounding the pavement, Bette found a job with a private investigator, who was no Sam Spade. Sadness seeped in around her panic when she thought about Spade's creator, Dashiell Hammett, dying only fifteen days ago in New York. Not in San Francisco, home of his greatest characters, Spade and the Continental Op. Walking the streets of San Francisco and the whole of the Bay Area through the pages of Hammett's stories made this particular city even more attractive. Nancy Drew, though still cherished as her childhood heroine, had been replaced long ago by the tough exterior covering the sentimental interior of hard-boiled detectives.

Her thoughts hammered away at her, depriving her of sleep as the neon lights on the corner flickered off and on through her window.

"No great job, no ocean view from my apartment, all my Hammett novels left with Sandy. To top that off, I nearly rented a room in the Thomas Hotel back in December. Twenty people died in that fire just three weeks ago. I could have been one of them. Then, I *would* have disappeared without a trace." Her own voice in the darkness made her shiver.

Still, she felt lucky. The Page Hotel was safer, if not cheaper, than the Thomas and closer to The Black Hawk. But it was taking longer than she expected to acclimate to the Bay Area winter. The fog and smoke seemed constant.

Defying the elements on Christmas Eve, she walked to the City of

Paris store to see the Christmas tree in the gorgeous rotunda. Sandy would want to hear about this amazing tree. When she wrote to Sandy after the New Year, Bette relished describing the tree and the rotunda, as well as the amazing Chinese Christmas Eve dinner she'd had along the way. Now, all that might be lost.

The memories of her first two months in the City and the potential for the loss of her freedom kept her tossing and turning. Yet Bette got herself up as usual for work the next morning and was sitting at her desk sorting the mail when her boss walked in around ten o'clock.

"Hey, Sweetheart, any calls or visitors?" Rod Butler, forty-ish, still solid, private eye.

"No, Rod, nothing since I came in at nine. Any luck on that surveillance last night?"

"Nah. I was bored stiff and shut it down around midnight. No one coming. No one going. I didn't see the point in staying up all night watching for his wife to come in or out of that shabby motel."

"Yeah, makes sense. Do you want me to call the guy?"

"Nah. I'll do that later. I just came in to check on calls and such. I'm heading out again for a meeting with a possible client. Catch ya later."

"Bye, Rod." Bette grinned and shook her head after he closed the door, knowing he was headed to the Embarcadero and the Old Ship Saloon.

Two weeks after she started working for him, she took her Shell map of the City and walked down Webster to Pacific during her lunch break. She meant to end up on Fisherman's Wharf gazing across the Bay at Alcatraz but missed a turn along the way.

That was five days before Christmas when the heavy fog and smoke had cleared long enough around noon for her to take a walk. Preoccupied with relatively fresh air, intermittent sunshine, and unfettered freedom, Bette forgot to turn left onto Polk toward the Wharf. Suddenly, she was at the Embarcadero looking out at Treasure Island instead of Alcatraz Island.

Oh, well, she thought at the time, what does it matter where I go in the City? It's all gloriously mine, by myself, alone.

She breathed in the salt air, turned around, and headed back down Pacific toward Butler's office on Webster.

In just a few steps, she realized she still needed to eat lunch. At Pacific and Battery, she thought she could grab a burger or something. When she stepped inside the Old Ship Saloon on that corner, she saw her boss, sitting on a stool at the far end of the bar clearly regaling his nearest neighbors with some story requiring the waving of his arms. She slipped out of the bar unseen.

Back in the office, she settled in to wait for his return as usual at four o'clock. She casually mentioned that a friend had recommended the burgers at the Old Ship Saloon. Did he know it?

He didn't question her about her so-called friend, even though he knew she had arrived in San Francisco only a short while ago. Instead, Butler told her that it was a private eye's duty to keep eyes and ears open in the neighborhood during the day. More clients would come his way if he positioned himself in the right spot. The burgers were the best.

The Old Ship Saloon near The Embarcadero, two-plus miles from their office, was hardly "the neighborhood" to a girl from small-town Oklahoma. But she was soon aware that this bar *was* a prime spot in the City for locals and tourists alike.

Bette took a few more lunchtime 'strolls' down Pacific to prove to herself that Rod Butler did, indeed, spend most of his days at the Old Ship, drinking and telling lies, his 'war stories', though he'd never been in a war.

At least that's what one of their chatty clients told her. He claimed Butler had been 4F, "unfit for military service" during the war. Butler himself never mentioned the war. She figured it was his business, like hers was her own.

Whatever his story is, she considered, he gave me a job, paying me enough every week to slow the dwindling of my savings. What little work there is, I can do with ease. Unlike Spade's Effie Perine, I haven't had to run any risky errands. But Rod Butler is no Sam Spade.

Bette also appreciated that Butler didn't ask for references or offer any other prying questions. At four every day, he wobbled back in from the Old Ship 'to get some paperwork done'. By the time she left at 4:30, he was asleep in his chair. Now and then, an interesting case even came his way.

As she thought about her boss, she realized that she might be able to ply him, discreetly, for information, find out how he goes about tracking someone down. Or maybe she could discover what she needed by a clandestine search through his case files. She checked her watch. 3:23.

Bette stepped out the corridor-door and peered down the hallway in both directions. Quiet. No one coming. She figured she had about thirty minutes to rummage through the files in his office to find something that might help her figure out how the Stalker had discovered her—not only in San Francisco but in her favorite jazz club a block from her apartment. Far back in one file cabinet, she found a smallish box. She couldn't help herself; she looked inside.

A Purple Heart lay on aging purple-cloth inside the box. Stunned, she held it almost too long. She managed to be back at her desk only two minutes before Butler sauntered in at four o'clock on the dot.

"How's it goin', Sweetheart?" He never called her by her name. She wondered if he remembered it.

"Fine, Mr. Butler. Did you get any new clients at the Old Ship today?" She teased, trying to prevent herself from asking about that Purple Heart.

"Of course, I did. Told ya. That's what I do there. Make myself available, for clients." He nearly tripped over his own feet trying to wink at her as he opened the inner door to his office.

"Tell me about the new client so I can prepare a file for him. Her?"

"Him. Name a' Smith. Or Smithson. Or something like that. Hang on, I wrote it down somewhere." Butler reached into the inside pocket of his rumpled suit coat, extracting a rather soiled cocktail napkin. "Here. See? Smith. Clemson Smith. What a handle, eh?"

After letting the napkin float down onto Bette's desk, Butler stepped through his door shutting it behind him.

Her hand shook as she pulled the napkin toward her and stared at her boss's sloppy handwriting. The name *Clemson Smith* scrawled across the middle of the napkin was clear enough.

"How did he find Rod at the Old Ship? Unless—" She clapped her hand over her mouth not wanting to hear her own conclusion spoken aloud.

What she heard instead was the scraping of Butler's chair and the squeak of his desk drawer being pulled out. He was about to have his afternoon shot of whiskey and then his nap. She was safe for a while. Bette shifted her eyes back to the scribble on the napkin and noticed that the name wasn't the only information there. Scrunched into one corner was a word and a number, Majestic 407.

"Think, Bette, think," she whispered to herself.

Her boss would be asleep by 4:30. Twenty minutes from now. All she had to do was wait, without screaming.

At 4:30 exactly, she put on her coat, grabbed her purse out of the desk drawer, and walked toward the corridor-door. As she reached for the handle, she heard footsteps on the other side, not far from the door. A sixth sense told her to hide. She stepped back and got down into the narrow space between the wall and the file cabinet. The door opened.

"Hello." She knew that voice. "Mr. Butler? Hello!" More demanding now.

"What? Who's there? Angel, is that you?" Butler's drunk sleep-fog slow to lift.

The man moved toward the inner door and opened it. Butler stood up and straightened his tie, his jacket and hat still laying where he'd tossed them on the client chair. The man narrowed his shark eyes.

"Mr. Butler, I wanted to follow up on our conversation at the bar this afternoon. May I sit?"

"Sorry, I had urgent business when I came in. And—" Butler cleared the chair. "I thought we were supposed to meet at the Old Ship tomorrow?"

The man interrupted. "Yes, well, my business is urgent, too. I have to get back home in a couple of days. Like I told you, I need to find my . . . sister. My folks are worried sick about her. She's impulsive. Doesn't know her own mind. You know how women are. She was supposed to be married before Christmas but disappeared right after Thanksgiving. I traced her to San Francisco with the help of my dad's counterpart here." Puffing himself up, "My father owns the daily newspaper back home. Last night, I found Elizabeth at a nightclub, of all places–drinking, and listening to *jazz music*." His upper lip curled. "Remember? I told you all that earlier today."

"Yeah, sure. I remember. My secretary's gone by now, but let me get a notebook and write this down. Tell me again why you didn't take that woman with you when you found her last night?"

The only response was something like a low growl through clenched teeth.

In the outer office, Bette had stopped breathing, her body frozen between the wall and the file cabinet. She wanted to hear more of what they were saying, but even more than that she wanted to get out of there. Far away from Clemson Smith.

She took a deep breath, rose slowly from her crouched position, and scooched sidewise along the wall. She removed her short-heeled shoes so they wouldn't clack against the old wood floor. Her stocking feet slipped a bit as she tiptoed toward the corridor-door. She eased the knob around so the latch didn't click. She was out the door, down the hall, and down the stairs before she put her shoes back on. She glanced over her shoulder at the stairs before stepping out of the building. Then she ran.

She didn't look back or try to catch a bus or hail a cab. She just ran as fast as she could while daylight faded from the City. She was certain that the other part of her boss's napkin scribble referred to the Hotel Majestic Room 407. Undoubtedly, Clemson's hotel and room number. He would have his luxuries.

Sometimes Bette walked by the Majestic on Sutter Street on her way home but decided it'd be safer to go the long way around today. She headed down Pine to Franklin to O'Farrell and then onto Leavenworth, all the while hoping the story of the Majestic's ghost girl haunting Room 407 was true. Bette silently begged the ghost to do something more than run water and make noises tonight.

Bastard, she thought. Now I can't go hear Tjader tonight at the Black Hawk. Or any night as long as Clemson's here. But how will I know when he's gone? Didn't he tell Rod he has to get back home in two days? How long's he been here? Has he been following me? The last thought sent an icy chill through her as she ran. She started calculating how long it would take her to pack up and leave San Francisco tonight.

Bette stopped running only when she reached her apartment. Her throat completely parched, she didn't bother to take off her coat but went straight to the bathroom sink for water. She drank a glassful and splashed more over her face. Then she sat down in the faded brocade chair.

If I hadn't taken every opportunity to explore the City these last two months, I wouldn't have gotten away today. Sure, I caught a bus a few times when it rained, but no more than that. No more San Francisco?

At this thought, she began to cry, tears of frustration and anger oozing down her cheeks. Her dream of living in California, in San Francisco with its steep hills, its twisting, turning streets, the Wharf, even Alcatraz had been realized. Was she going to let Clemson Smith take this away from her, too? Her tears ceased and her mind turned from reaction to action.

Bette realized she couldn't run away again. That would be ceding him control like he'd had since the first week of their relationship six months ago. A control so gradual, flattering, at the beginning. Little things. 'I can take you to the drugstore,' he'd offer. 'I'll go shopping with you', he'd declare. Soon, he wouldn't let her go out anywhere on her own. He checked up on her at work. Took her to lunch and dinner. But it wasn't loving attention.

She had been so proud of her independence, earning her own money, sharing an apartment with her best friend, Sandy. She had worked hard every day, always focused on her dream. Then she met Clemson. A fine diversion for a while, but once she started resisting his control, he got ugly. Vicious. Violent.

At first, a little push that he could pretend was playful. Then he threw a shoe at her when she wouldn't wear the ones he wanted her to wear. Then he grabbed her so hard it left a bruise on her arm. Then, one night, a man at a restaurant smiled at her and she returned his smile, innocent, polite. But after dinner, as they stood on her small porch, Clemson put his hands on her shoulders, as if to kiss her goodnight, but suddenly they were around her neck. Through bared teeth, he told her to watch herself giving away smiles to other men. Then he had the nerve, on Thanksgiving day with his whole family there, to announce their engagement. She had never agreed to marry him. She never wanted to marry anyone, especially not Clemson Smith. Within three days, she was gone.

Bette knew the danger she was in now that he had found her. Her workplace and even her favorite night spot weren't safe. She fully believed his meeting Rod at the Old Ship was no chance encounter.

Somehow Clemson knew. My only chance now is to escape. Not leave San Francisco. Not kill myself. But create a cleverly orchestrated deception. If Rod Butler will help.

Rod may be a lush and a somewhat pathetic private eye, she thought, but he's been decent to me. He might be able to convince Clemson that I jumped off the Golden Gate. Clemson's ego helping to convince him that I was overcome with shame for running away from him. I better talk to Rod before Clemson wins him over. The man's all charm and charisma when he wants something. It may already be too late.

But Bette had underestimated Rod Butler.

After the man left his office, Butler stayed, watching darkness creep into the City. He knew plenty of men like Clemson Smith. Men whose good looks and money delivered them anything or anyone they wanted. Butler recognized a vicious streak in this guy as well as who the man was really hunting.

Yeah, hunting, he thought, not searching for. Not his sister. Does he think I was born yesterday? Those shark eyes reveal the true cold-bloodedness of the man under his cool rich-boy exterior. He wants only one thing—to possess our sweet angel, our Bette. That's not gonna happen on my watch.

A knock on her door at ten o'clock that night sent Bette into a hyper state of panic. Her instinct propelled her up out of the chair toward the window where she could reach the fire escape.

All the corner rooms on the second, third, and fourth floors of the Page, like Bette's, had access. The Super had to show a new tenant the trick to release the last ladder to the ground. He had shown Bette. Once. Almost two months ago.

"Bette, it's me. It's Rod."

Relief. "I'm coming."

It only took her a few seconds to get to the door, even as she slowed herself down trying to calm her jangled nerves.

"Rod, I'm really glad to see you. I—"

"No time for niceties, Sweetheart. He's after you."

She didn't need him to explain. "I know. I was hiding in the office when he came in this afternoon. Then I ran while he was with you."

"Good. Listen, even though that big retainer he offered would be useful and I'm not sure what your story is with him, I know his kind. I won't help him find you. This is what you should do. First—"

But Bette cut him off, "I already have a plan."

Butler listened intently as she explained her plan. He nodded his head, willing to let her run her own con.

"That could work. Plenty of people throw themselves off that bridge. Plenty are never found. What about your family?"

"My neglectful parents split up long ago. No siblings. One real friend, Sandy, is coming out here as soon as she can. At least, she was. That's what she said in her letter."

"It's Saturday tomorrow, so just lay low for the next few days. I'll come by and tell you when he's gone."

"I'm sorry to involve you in all this. I'll tell you the whole story when it's over. Thank you."

"Don't worry about it. See you soon." Butler tipped his fedora to her and left.

Bette locked the door behind him, walked over to her small suitcase-style phonograph and put on the only jazz album she'd been able to bring, her favorite, "A Night at the Black Hawk."

"Since I can't go there tonight to see Cal Tjader live," she said to the room.

Bette sat down on the overstuffed chair, leaned back, and closed her eyes while the strains of Tjader's rendition of Basie's "Blue and Sentimental" washed over her.

On the fire escape outside her window, the man's shark eyes peered intently into the dimly-lit room while Bette, ignorant of his presence at the moment, began to relax.

A few minutes later, a faint metallic sound resonated over the fine notes of Jose Silva's tenor sax and stopped Bette's breathing. The hairs on the back of her neck tingled, and the sensation spread over the top of her head. She opened her eyes, but, as she got up out of the chair, she avoided looking directly at the window. She knew who was there.

Bette wanted to run, to scream, but she controlled her impulses. She willed herself to stop shaking. She stood and picked up her coat from the chair, acting as if she were about to hang it on the back of the door. With her body blocking the view between the window and where she stood, she held the coat up with one hand and unlocked the door with the other. Coat in hand, she bolted into the hallway running toward the exit that led to the parking lot on the south side of the building, an area that couldn't be seen from the fire escape.

She stopped, put on her coat, and eased open the outside door. No sounds disturbed the silence. A black '57 Fairlane, parked close to the door, gave her cover as she slipped outside. Help also came from the solitary light above the door, burned out as usual. The few street lamps this end of Leavenworth were obscured by the fog. The fog again would shield her as she started to run south on Leavenworth.

The fog that protected her also made it slow going at first. But, it was only half a block to Golden Gate Ave. She'd have to go the long way, avoiding Turk Street and The Black Hawk.

A light rain began falling, clearing the fog somewhat by the time she darted around the corner of Golden Gate and Gough heading north toward Pine.

When she escaped from her apartment, she hadn't thought beyond getting out of there, away from him. She realized help could come from only one person. She just hoped Butler would be at home in the apartment connected to his office on Webster, nearly two miles away.

It was midnight when she arrived banging on his door.

Nothing at first. Then, a groggy, angry, "Who the hell is it?"

"Rod, please. It's me, Bette, your secretary." She wanted to make sure he knew her.

"What are you doing here? What time is it?" Rubbing his eyes, he opened the door.

"Not long after you left my apartment tonight, *he* came up the fire escape to spy on me, maybe do worse. He must have followed you. I don't know how he got up on the fire escape or what he thought he was doing. I didn't stay around to ask. I took off as soon as I heard a clang outside my window."

"You don't know it was him? You didn't look?"

"It had to be him. Who else would be there?"

"Plenty of perverts in this city, Sweetheart. Could have been a random peeper."

"No. I know it was Clemson. No coincidence in any of this."

"Alright, calm down. I'll make some coffee."

They were drinking coffee mostly in silence at Butler's small kitchen table when someone rapped loudly on the office door.

"Stay here," the private eye added.

Certain now of the identity of his late night visitor, Butler slipped quietly into his inner office through the connecting door from his apartment. The inner door was solid wood but the corridor-door had a glass upper with Butler's name and occupation painted on it. He had to open his inner door a bit to see the corridor-door.

A man's face was pressed against the glass so Butler carefully shut the inner door, moving back through the connector to his apartment. He found Bette standing in the middle of the floor shaking with fear and anger.

"It's him alright, but I never tell clients about my little apartment here. He'll go away soon."

Butler misjudged the extent of Clemson Smith's brass.

Considering Bette's next move, they heard another noise. The man had broken into the office and was clumsily rifling through desk and file drawers.

"What's he looking for?" Bette hissed, getting angrier by the second.

"Probably thinks he'll uncover something about you by ransacking my office."

Butler's office was sacrosanct. He hated anyone going through his things, professional or otherwise.

"Maybe we should call the police. Have him arrested." Hopeful.

"Maybe. Or I can call someone who might take care of this. Discreetly." Butler remarked.

He slipped quietly out of the kitchen to his nightstand, picked up the receiver on his phone, and started to dial. Bette waved her arms from the kitchen doorway to stop him.

He went back to the kitchen, "What is it?"

"I–I hate Clemson, but I don't want him killed!"

"What?

"I'm sorry. When you said someone could take care of this, I thought you meant—"

"You think *I'd* do that? Even if I had that kind of connection, I wouldn't kill him."

"I didn't know what to think. I—"

"I know some people who could stop his pursuit, non-violently. A little sleight of hand at his hotel."

"What do you mean?"

"The hotel dick at the Majestic owes me. A few compromising pictures at the hotel with, um, an associate of the dick."

"You mean take pictures of him in bed with a prostitute?" Bette scoffed. "That would never work. He's too fastidious."

"Ah, but the beauty of this plan is that your 'ex' wouldn't have to actually be *in flagrante*. The hotel dick knows a photographer who could doctor up some images so it *looks like* he is. Smith doesn't have to do anything but be in his hotel room. The photo genius will do the rest."

"I say no more schemes. I'll just have to face him in broad daylight, in public. Of course, someplace where he can't lash out at me. Maybe at Macy's on O'Farrell or, better still — the lunch counter at Woolworth's on Clay and Polk. Woolworth's is so far beneath *his* dignity that he'd never make a scene there. Then he could convince himself he'd made a lucky escape not marrying such a low-class woman!"

"O.K. But would he come? And, if he did, would you be safe?" Butler frowned. "I should be there in the store."

"As long as he doesn't see you, but I'm sure that Woolworth's will neutralize him. And there's always plenty of people there, especially on a Saturday. Please, call him first thing. Tell him you found me, and I said I'd meet him. But only at Woolworth's lunch counter. One o'clock. And be sure to get that retainer from him first." Bette was a smart girl.

As soon as they were sure that Clemson Smith was long gone, Rod Butler drove her home.

By 12:30 the next day, Bette was sitting on a stool at the Woolworth's counter sipping a coke. She knew Clemson Smith would try to intercept her before she could get inside to the counter if she arrived too close to one o'clock. Around 12:45, Bette saw Smith arrive and begin to pace back and forth in front of the store. She didn't know that they were both under surveillance. Rod Butler had fulfilled his promise to contact Smith but also decided to take no chances considering what Bette had told Rod about Smith's threats to her physical well-being and Smith's antics in Rod's own office. Consequently, Butler positioned himself inside Woolworth's even before Bette arrived. He wanted to be near enough to the lunch counter to watch what happened when Clemson Smith showed up but far enough away to remain undetected by either

Bette or Smith.

Bette continued to sip her coke while keeping an eye on the pacing man just outside the door. Finally, at five minutes past one, Smith strode into the store. His eyes swept over the people starting and finishing their lunches at the counter. Then, he saw Bette. He was standing beside her fuming five seconds later.

"What do you mean by forcing me to come here to talk? Just come back home with me. I'll forgive your little escapade, obviously to make me prove my devotion. But, enough is enough. Stop this now." His tone was controlled but his shark eyes flashed.

"You might want to keep your voice down, Clemson. People are staring. You don't want Woolworth shoppers and diners to hear you, do you?" Bette knew she was baiting Smith's ego but couldn't help herself.

"This place is beneath *you* and, of course, *I* would never have set foot in here if you hadn't insisted. You know that, don't you? Oh, wait, that's why we're here!" Smith's control slipping.

Rod Butler, aware of the slippage, edged closer. Now he was just a feet away slouching in front of the candy counter, peering down along the lunch counter where people now openly stared at the man looming over the young woman at the far end of the counter.

"Yes, I know that and, yes, that's why I wanted to meet you here. We are through, Clemson. I don't trust you and never agreed to marry you. I am not coming back to Oklahoma. Ever. Don't try to contact me again! Is that clear?" Bette stayed seated but straightened her spine and met the shark eyes squarely.

"You'll come to your senses, now, Elizabeth!" Smith grabbed her arm but she was too quick, pulling herself neatly out of his grasp.

The moment Smith shot his arm out toward Bette's, Rod Butler nearly flew from around the candy counter. But stopped himself, gave her another few seconds while keeping his hand on the gun in his coat pocket.

"Grab me again, and I'll scream. Then, I'll ask this very kind waitress here to call the police. Your daddy's not here to save you." Bette's eyes moved from Smith's thundering face to where the waitress now stood nearby, hands on hips, eyes boring holes in Smith's head.

Smith's ego was taking a beating, the first of his life, in a store he always referred to as a place where 'only the unwashed masses congregated to eat their swill and buy their cheap trinkets'.

Without another word, Clemson Smith exited Bette's life.

By 8 pm on Valentine's Day, the smoke had lifted some, but the fog had taken up the slack. Rod Butler could hardly see a foot in front of him, but the Tenderloin had been his stomping grounds a decade ago. He knew the way.

When he walked in under the fluorescent light inside the door of the club, the small bald spot on the top of his skull glistened. He swiped his face with his handkerchief as the bouncer waved him through.

The minors were firmly ensconced behind the chicken wire perhaps more restless than usual. Butler had seen the new sign on the front entrance directing minors to the Hyde Street side door about ten yards or so down the block.

I used to be one of those kids until I earned my adult beverage pass at 21. Man, I heard Mulligan, Monk, Lady Day, Coltrane, Miles, Ellington, Dizzy, McRae.

Then, he realized that if Clemson Smith hadn't come in when he did on the night of January 26, forcing Bette to run out of there, her night would have been rudely interrupted anyway by the police raid at The Black Hawk. The cops or the mayor's attempt to ding the owners for underage drinking. Cost the owners some bucks, but the kids are still there. For now.

Has it really been almost two weeks since Bette ran to my apartment? And only slightly less since we flushed that turd from her life.

Butler mulled over the last week in his head until Cal Tjader stepped up to the mic and announced a surprise guest for the first song of Valentine's night.

Carmen McRae came out of the shadows singing "Lover Man." Butler listened until nearly the end of her song before he stood and saluted the singer with his glass. Then he turned his body toward the corner table, stage right and saluted two women there. One obviously excited, new to the scene, the other relaxed, serene, her dark auburn hair luminous in the dim light spilling out from the spotlight on the singer.

Rod Butler swallowed the last of his drink and walked through the smoke-haze to the front door onto Turk Street where the fog embraced him.

The Printer and the Professor

I

The man stood in the middle of the room. His eyes a piercing blue, his skin tone like weathered parchment beneath his soft cap of similar color, straight reddish-brown locks flecked with gray fell loosely to his chin. A leather apron covered a long-sleeved, wool top, sleeves pushed up above well-muscled forearms, ink-stained hands. His trousers were flannelled wool, tucked into leather boots. In each hand, he held an inking ball, its sheepskin top stained dark brown and dripping urine onto the rug. He was not smiling. Neither was Grace.

Grace's slight intake of breath, just shy of a scream, silenced her mantra of a name as the man glared at her.

The man was standing on her rug in the flesh, his reddening face evidence of the blood coursing through the veins bulging out on his forearms. All she could think at that moment was that it must be early morning where he is, was, has been, the dripping inking balls testament to their having been removed from the overnight urine bath. Or, perhaps, he was cleaning them at end of day before placing them back into the urine trough? Her scholar's mind trying to sort the details of this strange manifestation.

Grace had been repeating aloud the name of an early sixteenth-century printer she was investigating—only a slight research rabbit hole in the midst of her study of early modern occupations in York. The project was gaining momentum, coming to a place where she could finish her book and realize the culmination of four, long years of research and writing, while trying to make that mental leap across a cultural divide spanning five centuries. She wanted to be on speaking terms with these working people living in York in the 1530s.

But at that moment, she was enjoying the alliteration of just one name, the feel of it as her tongue lightly touched the roof of her mouth, air escaping from her lips, the sound as she strove to articulate what she understood as a Middle Dutch accent, the printer's name resonating in her head—Frederic Frees, Frees, Frees. The records declared him a "ducheman," admitted to the freedom of the City of York on 22 September 1496.

Today, 22 September 2020, a man, the spitting image of such a man as Frederic Frees, materialized in her study, dripping urine from printers' inking balls onto her rug.

"How . . . where . . . when—" she jumped up off the exercise ball which served as her computer chair. The slight slope in her floor allowed the ball to roll quietly but directly toward the figure of the man, stopping just shy of the tip of his boots. He backed away but only a half-step.

As she looked at this man, this apparition—what else could he be?—she wondered if she was losing her mind after all. Even as she had struggled and stressed over her work and life in general during these six months of pandemic lockdown, Grace always understood she was one of the fortunate ones.

"Who—" Grace stuttered.

"Nee!" he spoke.

"Oh, his accent is . . . but it couldn't be!! Real or imagined, that apparition has just spoken a word in Middle Dutch meaning 'No'! Or does it mean 'never'? Wait. Never is 'noit'?" Grace, quite used to speaking her thoughts aloud, especially over the last six months, contemplated the question.

The man cocked his head and folded his arms across his chest to signal the barrier he intended to impose between them. His movement caused the urine drip from his inking balls to increase their range across Grace's rug.

"Nee and noit to dripping, reeking urine!" She reached for the roll of paper towels she had used earlier to clean up spilled tea on her desk. That seemed a minor spillage now in light of the fetid stink of urine creating dark stains on her rug.

As she pulled off the towels, she moved toward him, squatted down, and began to mop up the drips. This caused the man obvious discomfort, but he didn't budge from his none-shall-pass stance.

"My Middle Dutch isn't up to a conversation, but—" she swiped away at the multitude of wet, foul-smelling spots and then rose from her squat.

"Where is?" the man shouted.

Grace now stood within inches of the man's face. "You just spoke English. What the—" she let the expletive die on her lips.

"Where have you brought me, witch?" his arms remained in place and his frown deepened even as he bent his head away from Grace's face.

"Nee, I am no witch. You brought yourself here. I—well, maybe I did bring you—No! You have to be a figment of my overwrought imagination, my desire to reach out and touch the past! That's why your English is intelligible to me. Although this stinking urine and the spots darkening my rug are no figment of my imagination. And your conceptualization of me? Definitely sixteenth-century. Obviously, my appearance wouldn't register with your ideas about women but—" Grace's would-be rant trailed off into intellectual speculation and then a sudden consciousness of her pandemic uniform—comfy jeans and sweatshirt (when not teaching online). "O.K. so, I'm wearing trousers," matching his glare and stepping back to create more space between them. "You are the result of six months of isolation and concentration on early modern—"

"Frederic Frees, stationer, bookbinder," one hand smacked his chest, and the inking ball in that hand sprayed urine even further across the rug. He dropped his arm to his side.

"*Did* I conjure you?" Grace stared back at him but softened her expression slightly before speaking again. "Grace." She made a similar, gentler gesture, pointing to her chest as she said her name. "I chanted *your* name three times after I found you in the Freemen's Roll for 1496, the year you were enfranchised in York and later when your son, Valentine, was admitted *per patres* for 1538. I found *your* name again in another document for 1505 when you were ordered by the mayor and council to reside at the Rose in Coney Street, and—"

"The Rose. Yes, I was there for ten years. My boys were born in the city, Englishmen they are. Were. They are dead now, my Valentine and my Edward, and I am dying because of it. My shop, robbed by the agents of the King. I have no more reason to live. Your name?"

"Oh, my name must be confusing. Rest assured, I am not a personification of the concept of Grace. My parents *gave* me the name Grace. And I called you here. I think. Or a vision of you." Wrinkling her brow, she went on, "I have read about you and your sons and daughters."

She didn't say daughters-in-law knowing he would not understand the distinction that term made. His son Valentine's wife and his son Edward's wife were, to him, daughters.

He looked wary at her statement. "I don't trust *any* English though your language and appearance are not like the English I have known, even in York. Ah, what does it matter now." He lowered his eyes and nearly dropped the still-dripping inking balls.

Grace wanted to tell him about her well-studied abhorrence of Henry VIII's vicious implementation of religious reforms but thought it best to simply say, "I'm so sorry for your loss."

"They are with God now. He alone knows the innocent from the guilty."

The urine drips were distracting her, "Can I put your inking balls in this bag?" As she spoke she pulled one of her stash of clear, plastic, archive bags out of a desk drawer, happy she had been able to keep so many from her last research trip to England.

He eyed the plastic bag suspiciously but nodded as he dropped his tools into the bag she extended toward him.

The dripping inking balls have weight! If *they are real*—the urine certainly is—then *he* must be real. She almost dropped the bag as this thought struck her, "You're alive, here, now in 2020?"

"Wat is 2020?" his English gave way to the influence of his likely Netherlandish origin.

A nightmare, she thought. But decided against such a witch-conjuring term, while she wondered if he might be Frisian. "A plague," she uttered.

"Ah. Do you have the pestilence yourself? That must be why you are alone here in this large inn." As he spoke he swiveled his head, and his eyes inspected every corner of her comfortable surroundings. "I am not afraid. If I get the plague, all the better."

"No. I do not have the plague. This is my study, my *bibliotheek*. The rest of my house is through that door. Do you want to come in?" Grace took a step to one side toward the door she was pointing at, smiling as she did.

"Nee." His voice said, but his face revealed intense curiosity.

She decided she would just start walking toward the door only a few feet away from where they stood. If he followed, they could sit down, have tea or—

"Bier?" she asked the dying man.

"Ja!" And he, too, began to move, to follow her through the door and into the main part of the house.

As they sat around her table drinking their beers, his eyes scanned the open living and kitchen areas. When he turned his neck to peer down the long hallway, he could just make out doors to other rooms. She was sure he couldn't fathom it all, but his early modern manhood demanded his silence in the face of his ignorance.

She asked him a direct question, "What did you mean when you said earlier that you were dying?" Though she was beginning to think he had the plague since his urine balls, now securely sealed, weren't the only things that reeked. His body odor was nearly overwhelming.

"I know that because I am in some kind of place between Heaven and Hell, not Purgatory. We do not believe in Purgatory, but this and you must be…somewhere."

"It is. I am. We are in Oklahoma." She watched him over the rim of her glass as she took another sip of beer.

"Oklahoom-a?

Grace wasn't sure how to explain where they were or who her ancestors were. "You wouldn't know where it was if I told you since this country had not yet been invaded when you were alive. I mean—"

"Invaded? Are you English?"

"No." Grace was not prepared to explain, even if he could comprehend her half Kiowa, half German ancestry.

"Goed." Frederic Frees drained his bottle of beer, then held it out at arm's length. "This is strange glass," he said as he turned the empty bottle around in his hand, "Very small." He sniffed and set the bottle on the table.

"Would you like another?" Grace had to restrain a laugh at his assessment of the quantity rather than the quality of modern beer.

"Ja."

As she walked to her refrigerator for another beer she realized that whether it had been morning or evening where he was (had been?), he might be hungry. "Are you hungry?"

"Ja."

Luckily that morning, she had picked up a grocery order, curbside, and yesterday had made a no-knead, seeded rye bread. She handed him the beer and walked back into the kitchen area, considering what food he would be inclined to eat. She knew bread and cheese would suffice while she pondered the possibilities of what else to feed this sixteenth-century man from York. Or, maybe originally, Frisia?

Grace pulled a chunk of gouda and the loaf of rye bread from her refrigerator, setting the wrapped cheese on her counter as she turned toward her oven. She set the proper temperature for warming the bread, placing the loaf on her butcher block to wait for the oven to heat up. She could feel his eyes watching every move she made but went on with her preparations, removing a bamboo cheese board from her cupboard before unwrapping the gouda and grabbing a knife from her countertop knife box. When she turned, cheese board and knife in hand, the man was, indeed, carefully scrutinizing her.

"I want to warm the bread, but we can start with some gouda," careful to give it the Dutch pronunciation, realizing as she did that modern Dutch (g)how-da might throw him as much as the standard American English goo-da. Never mind pronunciation, she thought, would this cheese have been available in York in the 1530s? Let's see—gouda originated in the twelfth century in the town of the same name near Rotterdam, but if he's not from the south and instead from Frisia or even the Frisian Islands…her thoughts trailed off as Frederic Frees put a large slice of cheese first under his nose and then into his mouth.

He smiled as he chewed. Grace returned his smile as an idea percolated in her mind. She reached in her pocket for her phone then thought better of it, turning around with her back to him before extracting it.

The shock of seeing me use this phone would definitely convince him that I was a witch, she realized. She continued to touch the screen until she had located the file she was searching for in her Dropbox—*Een notabel boecxken van cokeryen, A Noteworthy Book of Cookery*. The cookery book was printed in 1510 when Frederic Frees was already in York, and reprinted in 1514, by Dutch printer Thomas Vander Noot. Grace had recently acquired this electronic version, academic opinion being that whether Vander Noot had compiled the recipes or not, he certainly had printed them, twice.

I wonder if Frederic Frees knew Vander Noot, although the latter was in Brussels. Hmmm. Never mind. This little cookbook should give me some idea of what food might appeal to this very smelly figment of my imagination.

"Mistress Grace?" his voice cut through her study of the document on her phone.

Grace turned, surreptitiously returning her phone to her pocket as she did. "Uh, I'm just putting the bread in the oven for a few minutes to warm it through." And did as she said before walking and sitting down smiling, as if this were a regular occurrence—drinking beer on a Tuesday afternoon in Oklahoma in the year 2020 with a man from sixteenth-century York.

When the timer dinged fifteen minutes later, the man jumped a bit while Grace fetched the warm bread from the oven. With the bread on the butcher block, she cut off a few slices and then put the slices along with the rest of the loaf into a wicker basket, covering the lot with a blue cloth. As she carried the basket to the table, she caught Frederic Frees, stationer and bookbinder, again watching her.

He procured a slice of bread from the basket along with a fair-sized piece of gouda from the plate and spoke. "If I am to die here, tell me about this place. I see forest all around like in Germania, but you said this place is called Okiehomeia?"

"Oklahoma," her mouth poised over a slice of bread and cheese.

"Ja, Oklahoom-a. Is it an ancient place?"

"Yes, actually, it is," she began. Then thought that if she said—the forebears of her native ancestors found their way to this continent perhaps 80,000 years ago—he would return to the notion that she's a witch. So instead she said, "This land was ancient when my ancestors came here, a long time ago." She didn't think it advisable to discuss the bloody colonization thousands of years later by white Europeans flocking to this so-called New World more than a hundred years after *he* was born on another continent.

"Ah, your ancestors. The witches," he moved his head up and down knowingly.

"No, not witches," she sighed. "Just people like you and me." Trying to negate his persistent witch theory while confirming their shared humanity.

"If not a witch, then how do you warm bread without making a fire in your oven and what is that thing," he pointed to her refrigerator, "from where cheese comes cold wrapped in skin but also wax?"

Can I explain five hundred years of technological changes to this guy, she asked herself? Maybe I should take him outside. Oh, if we go outside of this house, maybe he'll disappear!

"Let's go outside and get some air. Alright?" Because you really stink and I'm sort of hoping you will vanish as quickly as you appeared. She smiled encouragingly at him.

The man frowned at her and then his countenance cleared. "Ja, let us go to the outdoors. I would like to walk a bit. Breathe."

Relieved, she stood up and headed for the door. He stopped.

"Wait. That does not go to the outside." His arms went back in none-shall-pass position.

"No, yes, well, we have to go back into my *bibliotheek* to get to the front door which will take us outside." She hoped this didn't seem too witchy.

"I see. Let us go then," as he spoke he uncrossed his arms and motioned to her to precede him out the door.

Wild thoughts skittered around in her head—when I reach the door and trip the latch, will he disappear? Will he remain trapped in the house like a spirit? Will I disappear? Will I regret losing him?

When they reached her study, she walked to the far corner where the front door now seemed far away. She took a deep breath as she reached for the handle and pressed down on the latch. The door opened, and she walked out onto her driveway.

Stopping abruptly, she turned, wondering if he followed or evaporated.

When she looked over her shoulder, she saw Frederic Frees exiting the house, pulling up short behind her abrupt stop.

"Oh, dear!" Expressing her surprise audibly made the man cross his arms again. "Sorry for stopping so quickly. I thought I—"

"Ja, you thought I would be frightened out here and would not follow you. But here I am. Wat is?" he cried, clearly alarmed by the sight of the vehicle that sat in her driveway.

"Let me show you," was all she could muster as she walked toward her 1968 VW Devon Motor Caravan, vintage, mint condition.

Frederic Frees followed her slowly, charting every move as she put her key in the lock and opened the sliding door to reveal the amazing interior of this special caravan bus—a cooker, water keeper, sink, cooler for food, electric lighting, tables, double bed, and more. Frederic Frees was transfixed.

A house on wheels, but what wheels were these, he wondered?

As if he were a prospective modern buyer, Frederic Frees from 1539, kicked the tire on its rubber surface, his leather boot bouncing off, almost propelling him backwards into Grace.

"Hey! Don't kick the tires, please. I'll try to explain them to you, but I don't know how productive a history of the evolution of tires would be right now." Grace's frustration was rising but not from the man's solitary kick to the Caravan's tire. Rather it was the fact that he was still there, in solid form, perfectly *able* to kick her tire.

"Let's go for a drive," she suggested, slyly watching his face for signs of fear? skepticism? deterioration of fleshy bits?

"Nee. We cannot transport ourselves in this little house." His masculine ego was showing.

"It's a caravan for transporting *and* housing people. Think of it as a fancy cart moving your goods and you from one place to another." She thought his skin was becoming translucent. She was sure he was fading and jumped when he spoke.

"I will go with you to see you safely there and back." He marched to the open sliding door and started to get in.

"Nee. Master Frees. You must sit up here next to me." Grace shut the slider and held the passenger door open with one hand while waving him in with the other.

After a few minutes of hesitation, disguised as contemplation, Frederic Frees climbed into Grace's VW Caravan and sat still, arms folded again across his chest.

"Here, let me help you with the seatbelt." She started to pull the belt across his folded arms. He vehemently resisted. "You have to wear a seatbelt. It's the law!"

"What do I care for laws of Oklahoom-a? Those of the English king killed my sons and daughters. Destroyed my life."

He has a point, Grace thought, so she stopped her efforts with his seatbelt and shut the passenger door.

Grace pulled her phone from her pocket and texted her friends while she walked around the back of the van. Frederic Frees was staring straight ahead, trying to look in control. As she plodded slowly around the van, Grace typed an emergency gathering message – **EMERG Alien visitor. Help needed.** Her three friends wouldn't hesitate to gather at Ruth and Phil's in the next fifteen minutes.

Climbing into the driver's seat, she put the key in the ignition and turned the engine over. Frederic Frees nearly came out of his seat. But, again, he controlled himself and settled for recrossing his arms tighter against his chest.

II

As she pulled out of her driveway, Grace wasn't sure this was a good idea. But as she drove down the street, casting side glances at Frederic Frees, struggling to maintain his sangfroid with the postmodern world rushing by him on all sides, to Phil and Ruth's to meet up with her Bubble felt essential.

Quarantine bubbles had been attempted early in the summer as people negotiated or rationalized their way out of loneliness and isolation from friends and family. Experts had come out divided on the benefits and dangers of such small group gatherings, people being the self-deceptive and recalcitrant social animals they are, but Grace had met twice during the summer with three of her closest friends. Like Grace, these friends were not your average folks. Ruth was a novelist, her husband, Phil, an actor, and, their mutual friend, Harry, a poet.

Phil and Ruth had hosted the two gatherings since they had a gorgeous deck with honeysuckle-covered trellises surrounding it, obscuring the sight and smell of any noisome neighbors while guaranteeing enhanced safety by being out of doors. The four friends lived close enough that no one was put out. Sadly, their quarantine bubble hadn't been repeated when the Covid numbers started rising again after the 4th of July. But *this* was an emergency.

When she pulled into her friends' driveway and turned off the engine, Frederic Frees replaced his shocked face with a highly suspicious one. "Wat is this? Am I arrested for not wearing this *sit belt*? Perhaps this is the Council's gaol?" Frederic Frees did not look at her as he spoke but straight ahead at her friend's dark, oak-paneled front door.

I have to admit, she mused, that door does remind me of the Bocardo Prison door in Oxford except Phil and Ruth's door has a lovely, leaded-glass window at the top.

Grace turned to her passenger sitting rigid in the seat beside her. "Nee, Master Frees. This is not prison. This is the house of my friends. We are making a call, a visit. Okay? I mean is that agreeable to you?"

Frederic Frees did not respond, his focus still on the door before turning his head side to side, scanning the area. Of course, no one was around since most people who could had retreated back into the relative security of self-isolation. Then a car pulled up behind them.

"Don't worry," she said quickly, noticing the renewed tension in his body, "That's just my friend, Harry. He's visiting, too."

Frederic Frees narrowed his eyes as he skewed his head toward Grace and then back to watch a tall dark-complected man with long, flowing, black hair stride up the driveway.

Harry stopped next to Grace's door and started to speak before he spotted the man sitting in her passenger's seat. Harry's face contorted with a series of expressions from quizzical to concerned. Grace, eyes wide, gestured him into the house with her head.

Comprehending her gesture, Harry continued on to Ruth and Phil's front door. Grace got out and walked around the Caravan to the passenger's side. Extending one arm to open his door, she could see the serious trepidation on Frederic Frees's face. Grace smiled and pulled his door toward her.

"They will have *bier* and more cheese," she smiled, relying on her friends' pre-pandemic hospitality with plentiful wine, beer, cheese, and assorted goodies and on Master Frees' curiosity or his desire for more beer.

"Ja? Goed."

Beer to the rescue again. Not surprising considering beer or ale was a staple in sixteenth-century York, Grace reflected. Radiating friendliness, she verbally maneuvered him out of the van and onto the driveway. Although he strode along beside Grace to the front door, Frederic Frees resumed his none-shall-pass stance while Grace knocked.

In just a few seconds, Phil opened the door, greeting them with the face of an angel, "Welcome to our house. We are so happy you are here today." Phil was a great actor.

For the first time since Frederic Frees had materialized in her study earlier that day, Grace reached out to touch the arm of this sixteenth-century anomaly to guide him gently into the house but pulled her hand back before she made contact.

Ruth and Phil were ready in spite of the short notice, always stellar hosts and adaptable to any situation. Introductions and distribution of bottles of beer began as Frederic Frees, still exuding the stench and filth of his print shop (urine, ink, and unwashed body), giving up his crossed arms only long enough to grab the beer he was handed.

"It's such a lovely day. Let's go out on the deck," Ruth, beautiful and kind, meant to encourage the stinky man out of the house, to keep safe distance between us all.

"Let's," Phil pulled open the sliding glass door to the deck, while Ruth continued to smile at Frederic Frees, gesturing to him to follow them out the door.

Laying her phone on the kitchen counter, Grace grabbed the cheese and fruit plate while Harry followed with the small ice chest full of beer. Everyone was now on the deck situating themselves in chairs set at a distance around a large round wooden table. Except for Frederic Frees.

"Nee. What is that?" he asked, having stopped forward motion at the door to the deck while pointing toward the tiny house in the far corner of the yard.

"That's Ruth's writing studio," her husband smiled, proud of his wife's achievements.

"She is a textwriter? I never met a woman textwriter. Only men." Stubborn in his sexist proclivities, Frees frowned in the direction of the rest of the bubble.

"I'm a novelist, a writer of—" but Ruth was stumped momentarily to explain novels to a man whose existence preceded the genre. "Prose."

"Ah, like the Alexander books. History. You are a scribe." Frees nodded knowingly.

Harry interjected, "Yes, Alexander books. Some were prose works, but some were in verse. That's what I do. I write verse. Poetry."

Frederic Frees cocked his head but finally put his arms down to his sides as Grace spoke, "Master Frees. Come. Sit and be comfortable. Have another *bier*," she pronounced the last word as he would have done, trying still for a kind of camaraderie.

Grace and her three friends were relieved when Frees walked out of the house and sat down in the empty chair. Harry handed him another cold beer and pushed the cheese and fruit plate in his direction.

"I am most grateful." Frederic Frees took a long, slow drink emptying the bottle. Then he bowed his head. "For all of you, I wish God's grace...grace...grace." As the last word faded, he vanished.

"What the hell just happened?" Harry's chair toppled over as he leapt up out of it.

Phil was already off the deck and into the middle of the yard turning in a circle, searching with his whole body. "He's not here."

"Grace, what *is* going on?" Ruth, normally rational and calm spoke with a decided edge to her voice.

"I can't. Well, perhaps, I can. I knew what would follow when he started with 'I wish' and while he was repeating that word, my name, I was repeating, under my breath but aloud, his name."

"You'd worked out how this came about then?" Phil had just come back up on the porch, unconsciously pulling his hair up into a peak as he spoke.

"When he appeared in my study, I had just repeated his name three times from an entry in my notes. *Poof*, he stood in front of me with those damnable inking balls dripping urine on my rug. I didn't know if my repeating his name as he said mine—for him the concept of grace—would work."

"What inking balls? You have to tell us the whole story now!" Harry was setting his chair to rights.

"Yes, please!" Ruth and Phil in unison.

Grace proceeded to tell her tale of the apparition called Frederic Frees. Although they could see the two empty bottles the man had left behind, his presence, their conversations with him, Grace's story, everything seemed fantastical. They talked late into the evening before Grace realized that the shock and excitement of the day had taken its toll.

"Maybe we had a shared hallucination," she offered as she stood at the front door preparing to leave.

"Maybe. But I'm definitely getting a poem or ten out of this," Harry had been scribbling on a small notepad for the last hour as their conversation wound down.

"I'll beat you by a novel, Harry," Ruth teased. "I took notes, too!"

"I have a new character to bring to the stage," Phil said as he folded his arms across his chest and glared with only a slight smirk.

"Thank you all for talking me through this bizarre whatever-it-was. I'm going back home to sleep." Grace smiled and waved but said to herself...I hope.

Grace's drive home seemed longer than usual in the dark, autumn night, an emotional hangover vibrating throughout her body.

Fifteen minutes later, she pulled up to her house, turned off the ignition. She leaned back in the seat, the spectre of Frederic Frees lurking in the empty seat beside her. Grace forced herself out of the

Caravan and up to the door. But as she turned the key in the lock, she realized she was expecting to see Frees standing in the spot where he had appeared in her study just hours before. Or was she *hoping* to see him there?

Was it really a pandemic hallucination shared with my three closest friends? Maybe I've been dreaming? As her scattered thoughts continued, Grace moved further into the large room, her body tensed, expectant as she flipped on the overhead light.

"No one's here. Just me. As usual," she laughed nervously as she placed her bag onto the hook on the wall. "But, oh, I should have asked him so many questions. So little is really known about him. And what he could have told me about printing in York, about the abominations of Henry VIII!"

Deflated, Grace switched off the light before opening the door that led to the rest of her house. But as she did, the fading light in her study reflected off of something on the floor by her desk. Before the room could go completely dark, she flipped the light back on.

Her eyes refocused in the light and jumped to the floor by her roll-top desk. A plastic bag rested on the rug there, the bottom of it bulging out, darkly stained.

Grace moved slowly forward, never taking her eyes off the bag. She reached down and plucked it from the floor, its weight substantial. Then, she switched on the floor lamp next to her desk. The circle of light it created shone like a spotlight on the rug with its scattering of dark stains and on the plastic bag she held at arm's length.

Inside the plastic bag, two sixteenth-century printer's inking balls smeared the interior with black ink and urine. Grace reached into her jeans' pocket for her cell phone. It wasn't there.

The Nun's Curse

Standing inside the main hall of their mother's ancestral home sur-rounded by peeling wallpaper, a cracked stone floor, and the coldest December chill they had ever known, Kate Thornton's children, Peter and Lily, ages 10 and 12, couldn't understand why they were in this drafty, old wreck of a house in a small, boring village in Yorkshire. But, barely a year after their father was murdered outside a tube station in London, where they had lived all their lives, here they all were. As her ancestors had done before her, Kate Thornton was determined to restore the old house to life one more time. In spite of the curse.

Kate had never breathed a word to her children about the supposed curse on the Thornton ancestral home. But weeks before he died, Kate's father told them about it. And the pub, where Kate and the children had taken rooms for their first weeks in the village, only served as a reminder of her father's lapse in judgment. The pub bore the name, The Nun's Curse.

Family legend and local history agreed on one fact. When Henry VIII's northern minions drove the nuns out of the local convent in the late 1530s, the last prioress had laid a curse on the buildings and grounds. In what manner or words the curse was laid became fare for the would-be scops of subsequent ages. As with all religious houses at that time, this one, too, was intended to be sold to either one of Henry VIII's favourites or a gentry family who could afford to bribe Cromwell

"

or his local agent.

The Thornton family patriarch, having a manor nearby, had deftly outmaneuvered his neighbors and the Crown to take possession of the nunnery's buildings and grounds, known locally after that as Priory House. In acquiring the material possessions of the nunnery, in spite of remaining faithful to the Old Religion, the family acquired the curse.

Locals, as well as folks throughout the county, had depended on the nuns' charity and prayers, as well as the work the convent could provide. They were satisfied that this stolen property, as they saw it, had been cursed. And, as the former beneficiaries of the nuns, they felt justified in removing what building stones and other bits and bobs that remained on the grounds. At least until one local man, carrying some of the purloined stones in a satchel, stopped off at the public house, wandered quite drunk toward his home on a very dark night, and, crossing a stile near Priory House, let his satchel's shoulder strap slip onto the stile post. He was found the next morning strangled by his stone-filled satchel. Belief in the curse revived, and no one picked up so much as a pebble from the place after that.

Because of this history, the village naturally felt obliged to disparage the Thornton family for bringing the curse back with them from London. Since Peter and Lily had to go to school in the village, the local children, no doubt fueled by their parents' and their own outlandish versions of the curse legend, ostracized and tormented Kate's children.

Peter came home the first day of school in January holding back tears, "Mum, they're monsters! Two boys started chanting and got others to do it, too, while I was eating my lunch by myself not bothering anyone."

"What did they chant?" Kate kept her voice calm.

"Cursed, cursed, cursed! Thorntons leave now!"

"Hmph, I didn't let the bumpkins at my school get to me even though they whispered and sniggered as I walked down the hall," Lily exclaimed almost convincingly. The older children in Lily's secondary school being more subtle while still being cruel.

Even though Kate had been born in this village and spent her first years here, she, too, had met a cool reception. At the green grocer's, the baker's, or wherever she went, she was directly cut or barely acknowledged by everyone, including clerks and proprietors. The owners of the pub, the Farleighs, were unfailingly polite but not friendly. Kate now understood the real reason she had refused for all these years to even visit this place.

When his job as a barrister or the stress of the City would get to him, her husband, George Carlyle, would float the idea of chucking their jobs, leaving London, and taking a crack at restoring Kate's ancestral home. Kate always had good reasons to stay in London—the kids' schools, their jobs, George's parents in Ealing. The morning before he was murdered, George had brought up moving again, Kate poo-pooing the idea. After he was stabbed that night trying to break up a fight between two youths outside a tube station near his chambers, Kate tortured herself with the unforgiving "what if."

What if I'd given George his way when he told me he wanted to leave London? Mightn't he have come home earlier or met me without taking his usual route? He could still be alive, if only, that morning, I'd agreed to the move. Is that why I dragged us back to this desolate place? Does a curse follow you from place to place?

"Mum, where are you?" her children's voices broke through Kate's negative musings. They possessed an uncanny ability to call out to her at the same exact moment, even when in different rooms.

"Here, in the kitchen, choosing paint," Kate called back, trying to convince herself that she had actually been considering the paint samples lying on the table in front of her.

Peter and Lily came running into the kitchen from opposite directions, stopping abruptly at the table to stare at the samples.

"Mum, these colors are rather . . . boring, don't you think?" Lily, the Critic.

"Only a few rooms aren't stone walls and need painting, right?" Peter interjected as his mother narrowed her eyes at his sister.

"Yes, the upstairs toilet and the bedrooms." Kate shuffled all the samples together as if they were a deck of playing cards. "Pick a card, any card, you two. And don't look at your card yet. Turn it upside down right here." Kate pointed to a cleared spot on the table.

Still young enough to enjoy any kind of game, the children each grabbed a sample card and promptly turned the cards upside down in front of their mother.

"Right. This one, Peter," she pointed to her son's card, "will be your bedroom's wall color. And this one," pointing to Lily's card, "will be yours. Now, turn them over." She expected to hear groans and complaints immediately and was surprised at the initial silence while the children looked at the two cards.

"Hey, that's not bad," Peter finally said.

"Mine's OK, too," Lily grudgingly admitted.

"Good, that's settled then." Kate started to pick up the sample cards when Lily reached out to stop her.

"Oh no, Mum. It's your turn now. Pick two, no three cards. One will be the upstairs toilet, one your bedroom, and the other Nan's room." Both watched with devilish glee as their mother picked three cards and turned them upside down next to the others before flipping over first one then another to display the colors.

"Crikey, I think I can live with these as well! Butter yellow for the loo, lapis lazuli blue for my room, and this rosy bougainvillea for your Nan's room," Kate smiled. "Let's fix dinner."

By mid-February, the rooms were painted and the restoration had moved to what they now uncreatively dubbed the North Wing. The weather seemed to warm up a bit along with the atmosphere in the village. At least, Peter and Lily each had made one friend and were about to bring those friends home after school for the first time.

Kate was surprised at her own nervousness. It's hardly the first time the children have brought friends home, she told herself.

"But," her voice echoing in the empty house, "it's the first time for *village* friends to come."

She had bought two varieties of chocolate biscuits and made a nice pot of tea for their arrival. Kate was setting the table when she heard the small gang of children burst through the door.

"Mum, we're here," Peter announced with great energy.

"In the kitchen," Kate found herself wondering vaguely if these village children would have horns and tails as Peter and Lily had asserted about their peers during the first weeks of school.

The two older girls sashayed into the kitchen with the two boys lagging along behind them. "Mum, this is *my* friend, Charlotte."

"Mum, Freddie. Freddie, Mum," said Peter, eyeing the biscuits and tea.

"Hello, welcome to our home, Charlotte and Freddie. Tea and biscuits here for everyone." Kate felt her nervousness rise again as the two guests stared at her.

Maybe they expected *me* to have horns and a tail, Kate thought. Peter tugged his friend's jumper guiding him to a chair, then started pouring tea into cups. The others grabbed biscuits for their plates. Kate could always rely on Peter to defuse social tension. Lily and Charlotte sat down in queenly fashion but were soon lost in the consumption of tea, biscuits, and pre-adolescent gossip.

Relieved, Kate left them to it while she went into the sitting room to build the fire in anticipation of the chill night air that would start to seep in around the stone walls as the sun set.

The pleasant day receded and gentle snow started falling shortly before the two new friends were to head home. By the time children and coats were fetched from various parts of the house, the gentle snow had turned into an unexpectedly fierce snowstorm.

I can't let them walk home in this cold, wet mess, and I certainly don't want to drive in it, Kate thought as she peered out the front windows.

She had been planning to let Peter and Lily walk their friends home and then have supper in front of the television, an unexpected bending of house rules. After that, she would concentrate on some paperwork while the siblings assessed the success of their friends' visit and prepared for bed. The snow upended her plans as well as threatened the safety of her charges.

Peter managed to resolve his mother's dilemma, "We could call their mums and ask if they could stay the night?"

"Mum, it's Friday, after all," Lily, brows arched in preteen challenge, "and half-term next week."

"That's fine with me. Do you two want to stay—" Kate began.

"What if we get the curse on us?" Freddie interrupted, eyes widening.

"Don't be childish," Lily chastised, offended. "The stories are fun to listen to, like ghost stories. But like the ghosts in those stories, the curse is not real."

Charlotte remained silent, clearly torn between her friend's assertions and the sparks of the long-held fear of Priory House, especially aggravated by night coming on.

Peter the Negotiator devised a solution. "Let's call your mums and see what they say about staying over. If the answer is yes, then, obviously they don't think there's a curse."

Freddie seemed to mull this over and then nod in agreement. Charlotte hesitated, "Well, I'm sure my parents don't believe in curses and ghost stories, but they may have something for me to do in the morning." She was hedging her bets.

"Great! Cheers." Kate clicked off from the last call and turned to the four anxious faces. "You both can stay over."

The boys immediately went running upstairs to Peter's room, but Charlotte, standing next to Lily appeared a bit gobsmacked. Lily had to nudge her before she would move.

Kate's feelings focused now on finding something intriguing to feed *four* hungry children before getting on with whatever she might be able to accomplish of the work she originally planned for tonight.

After supper in front of the television (a special concession) followed by some board games, the four trooped off upstairs to prepare for bed and lights-out whispering. Kate leaned back on the sofa in front of the fire, feeling more tired than she expected. Sighing with relief as she put her feet up on the hassock, she was about to close her eyes when a shriek rent the silence. She jumped up, instantly heading for the stairs.

"Peter! Lily! What's happening?" she called trying to keep the edge of fear mixed with anger out of her voice.

When she reached the landing at the top of the stairs, Kate saw Charlotte standing in the middle of the recess between the two walls of bookshelves. The child was visibly trembling as Lily draped a cardigan around Charlotte's shoulders. The boys moved closer to Kate.

Three antique leaded-glass windows were set in the stone wall in the recessed area with two more bedrooms and the loo beyond. Kate could see snow still falling heavily but nothing else.

"Are you all right, Charlotte? Are you ill or hurt?" Charlotte seemed to want to speak but was having trouble. Kate felt more distressed as she tried to comfort the girl. "Charlotte, talk to me. What is it?"

"I saw . . . something, a figure cross the floor over there." Charlotte pointed toward the hallway where the upstairs toilet was.

"All of you stay here while I investigate." Kate smiled reassuringly, particularly for Charlotte's benefit, and headed down the dark hallway past the recess, pushing the button on the light switch to illuminate the area as she went. At the end of the hall, she turned into the loo, pulling the chain for the light.

She was speaking as she came back into the hallway, "Nothing and no one here. I'm sure it was only a trick of the light through the windows there. Let's go down stairs and make tea with lots of sugar for everyone. OK?"

Kate smiled at Charlotte again and gave her daughter a look that said, 'help me out here.' Lily responded silently by putting her arm around Charlotte and guiding her toward the stairway. Peter and Freddie ran down ahead of the girls. Kate started to turn off the lights upstairs but decided to leave them for their return after tea.

Tea duly made and imbibed, the four friends proceeded back upstairs, Charlotte stopping to use the toilet off the kitchen. Kate picked up cups, saucers, and spoons and rinsed them in the sink.

"I'll wash these up in the morning," she proclaimed to the empty kitchen.

If Kate could have confessed to anyone at that moment, she would have admitted that Charlotte's scream and her "something, a figure" had made her own skin crawl. She didn't believe in curses or ghosts, but Priory House's cold, stone floors and walls with the oversized, eighteenth-century, leaded glass windows might conjure either, especially for a child whose head was filled with tales of a curse.

I do hope this is not a setback for the children's new friendships or cause for renewed antipathy in the village, she thought, walking around the room picking up the board games and contemplating the potential fallout from the evening.

As she put the games in the chest beneath the ground floor's identical old windows, Kate felt a prickling at the base of her skull. She saw someone, not something, move with speed away from the window as she stood up from closing the chest. The anger that rose up countered the cold chill of surprise, and she headed for the front door, grabbing her coat and snatching up her late husband's cricket bat from the ancient umbrella stand.

A floodlight on the front side of the house now shone on the white snow, revealing fat flakes falling. Kate felt momentarily disorientated, but her natural protective instincts aligned with her anger, urged her away from the mammoth oak door, now shut behind her. Kate stepped onto the path around the side of the house striding deliberately toward the garden below those windows. Because of potentially slippery ground, she moderated her pace and her temper. The last thing she wanted was for those snoops to discover her flat on her arse in the snow.

Coming slowing round one side of the house, Kate readied her bat. But whoever had been there was gone. She pulled her small torch from her coat pocket, switching it on to shine along the ground in front of the windows. She spotted footprints there, but the snow still falling was already covering them up.

She bent over, directing the light at one of the prints to see if the size or texture could tell her anything. As she did, Kate heard giggling on the other side of the porte-cochère. Conscious of the slippery ground, she moved nimbly but carefully toward the sound, shadowing her torch as she went. Easing along the stone wall on the house side of the porte-cochère, she reached the opposite archway and threw the light of her torch onto three teenage intruders in hoodies, mouths agape, and thoroughly surprised.

"You'd better start running before I put a curse on you along with this bat on your backsides," Kate shouted, standing like Diana, only with cricket bat waving in the air instead of bow and arrow.

The only reply, feet flying across snowy ground, slipping, sliding, and falling from time to time as the three interlopers ran toward the village.

In the morning, I'll tell the children that Charlotte's "something, a figure" was actually the shenanigans of teenagers messing about out here. They must have waved their own torches around, creating light and shadow through those big windows.

Kate ground her teeth as she walked more slowly through the still-falling snow back to her front door. Then she decided she'd better check that those hooligans hadn't disturbed the scaffolding on the exterior of the North Wing.

Finally back inside, she hung up her coat and deposited the cricket bat into her father's old umbrella stand. For some reason at that moment, the cricket bat among the umbrellas relieved her anger and frustration and almost made her laugh as she headed back to the fireplace to regain her composure and dry the cuffs of her trousers.

The next morning, Kate related her encounter with the teen intruders. They all listened intently, their expressions changing quickly from wide-eyed discomfort to satisfied smirks. Charlotte and Freddie even offered the names of local teens they suspected of making the unwelcome visit. After that, the four gobbled up their breakfast before running outside to look for footprints, making a winter game in the snow. Kate's warning to steer clear of the scaffolding followed them out the door.

When snow fell in London, it rarely remained long on the ground because of the chalk deposits beneath. Consequently, Peter and Lily were especially delighted by the mounds of snow that had fallen overnight, now reflecting bright sunshine. A perfect day for playing mindless games until the dampness and the cold brought them back inside for more food and hot drinks. Around 3:00, it was time for Charlotte and Freddie to go home.

Of course, Peter and Lily lobbied for another night with their friends, reasoning that since it was half-term no school work loomed. Kate gracefully refused so that neither the two guests nor her children were insulted or upset. A promise was secured for another overnight before school resumed.

Peter and Lily walked Freddie and Charlotte through the village and then ran home quickly to avoid getting caught out in the chilly, early winter twilight. Prowling teenagers aside, neither Peter nor Lily wanted to encounter the skulking ghost of a nun cursing in the darkness.

No more night visitors appeared that week or at any time before the Easter holiday arrived in late March. Kate looked forward to two full weeks of numerous house projects to keep them all busy, while she kept a watchful eye on the restoration of the North Wing. At any rate, that was Kate's plan when her children came home from school the day before the holiday began.

"MUM!" Peter was howling before he was halfway through the front door.

His sister contributed to the untamed chorus, though with pre-teen dignity, "Mum!"

Oh, no, Kate's brain started ticking off what problems might ensue—renewed harassment at school, sibling argument, dissolution of friendships. She sighed and went toward the uproar.

"What is it?" her tone was less, 'Welcome home,' and more, 'Now what'?

That stopped the two in mid howl as they dumped satchels and coats on the hall tree, a splendid Victorian antique, one of the few family heirlooms from Kate's father.

"Mum? What's wrong?" Peter, as always, sussing out a potential family crisis to negotiate.

"Nothing, my darlings. I was deep in thought. You startled me. That's all. What is it?"

Of course Lily, as the eldest, was their spokesperson, "We have invitations for the holiday break. Can we go?

"Please, Mum," Peter's gentle pleading usually worked better than his sister's whinging.

"First, you have to tell me *who* invited you and *where* they want to take you and for *how long*." Kate felt strangely uneasy.

"To London, dear London. The Farleighs," Lily rhapsodized out of order.

"Only for a couple of days." Peter's instincts concerning his mother's moods being usually spot on.

Her eyebrows cocked, Kate stared at her children's faces, filled with longing, and readied herself for the battle of London. "The Farleighs who own the pub?"

"Yes. Their son is in Peter's class, and their daughter is in mine. We're *friends*!" Lily said the last word with great emphasis.

"What happened to Charlotte and Freddie?" Kate had to ask.

"Freddie and I are planning a ramble when I get back." Peter volunteered. "If that's alright with you, I mean."

"Charlotte and I are not really friends any more. She's too nervous for me and never invited me to her house after *she* came here ages ago." Lily sniffed and rolled her eyes as if the absence of an invitation from Charlotte was nothing to her.

Kate knew better and was sorry that it was Charlotte who first encountered the midnight intruders as a ghostly image on the upstairs wall. She hadn't met the Farleighs' children except briefly during her family's stay at the pub. But during that time, none of the Farleighs had been any more than business friendly.

"Well, I want to meet parents and children again before I agree to this." Kate's stone face, as the children called it, brooked no rebuttal.

But they were well-prepared. "We're invited tonight to have our tea at the pub and talk it over," Lily beamed triumphantly, proud of her local linguistic knowledge. Peter smiled cautiously.

"You mean supper? What time?" Kate's face remained unchanged.

"Half six," Peter and Lily declared simultaneously.

"All right. Pick up your satchels and coats and put them away. Then, come have tea and biscuits and tell me more." Kate maintained her stone face as she walked to the kitchen to put the kettle on.

By quarter past six, Peter and Lily were chomping at the bit to go. Kate wasn't best pleased with the sketchy plans they had proposed. After all, their time in their respective schools was a little less than three months, and, although the Farleighs were local business owners of long-standing in the village, she didn't really know them.

Why go to London for the Easter holiday? Then Kate remembered having to push through the hordes of frenzied Easter tourists in London. *Everyone,* apparently, went to London for Easter.

She also had a suspicion as to how this particular trip probably came about. If her two became friendly with anyone, they would be asked about their lives in London. Kate stopped thinking about how they got to this point to prepare the questions she would be asking the Farleighs.

Mr. Farleigh walked out from behind the bar as soon as their guests arrived and deftly, but cheerfully, steered them into a small private room off the main public area. The table was nicely laid out, with a little glass vase of freshly picked daffodils in the center. Kate was still uncomfortable but smiled genially as Mrs. Farleigh and her two children came into the room from another door.

"Mrs. Carlyle, we are so happy to see you again and to have this chance to chat about the children's scheme." Mrs. Farleigh was apparently as taken aback by the announcement of the trip to London as Kate herself. So Kate didn't correct the "Mrs. Carlyle," trying instead to mask her irritation at Mrs. Farleigh who knew Kate's surname perfectly well.

"Call me Kate, please," she smiled. "Thank you for having us tonight. A fun start to the Easter holidays." Kate hoped her smile *passed* for genuine.

"Lily and Peter have told Emily and Jack all about London life and their eagerness to show them their favourite places." Mrs. Farleigh's strained smile gave way a bit as she added, "I'm Jean."

"Well, Kate, you know how excited the young ones are for Easter holiday. We thought we'd take the train down tomorrow and wander around a couple of days. These four'll be tired out by then." Mr. Farleigh flashing his genial-pub-host smile.

While the four children dove into their fish and chips and steak and kidney pies steamed in front of the adults, Kate started her interrogation.

"Where do you plan to stay in the City, Mr. Farleigh? Do you have family there?"

"It's Reg, Kate. My cousin manages the bar at the Hilton on the Bankside. He was able to get us rooms there at a good price." Reg Farleigh was ready for the examination. "Close to Tube and rail stations so we can be off anywhere in a flash. Your two claim to be expert at getting around in London."

Was that a criticism of her parenting? Kate shrugged off the imagined reproach with a soft laugh. "Yes, they like to think of themselves that way, but they weren't allowed to run about on their own. Their father or I was always with them." She hadn't meant to mention her dead husband, but there he was.

"Ah, we were sorry for your terrible loss." Jean Farleigh's sincerity was genuine.

Kate relaxed a bit as she thanked her for her sympathy and steered them back to London. "Lots to see on the Bankside and easy access on the other side of the river as well. Have you spent much time in London yourselves?"

The adults stepped gingerly away from the spectre of Kate's murdered husband and nattered on about the myriad of London excursions. The four children sitting at one end of the table, now eating their pudding, were obviously conspiring, plotting their own itinerary for the next two days.

When Kate and her children left for home later, the London trip had been approved and arrangements made for the next day's departure. Kate felt apprehensive about Lily and Peter going back to London without her but couldn't bring herself to refuse them.

Her children were uncharacteristically quiet as they walked back across the village to Priory House. The minute the door closed behind them, they ran to the staircase yelling, "We have to pack!"

I do understand that I have to let them have experiences without me, even as I burrow into this old patchwork of a house, she mused. It's only for a couple of days. I should revel in the quiet.

The next morning was far from quiet until Lily and Peter and their bags had been deposited with the Farleighs. Kate walked home trying not to feel anxious about the children's trip. After all, she reasoned with herself, they spent their whole lives in London before coming here. They've learned how to be cautious. I hope.

Their father, a criminal defense barrister, had once caught Peter and Lily pouring over crime scene photos that were pretty ghastly. That happened six months before he was murdered on his three-minute walk from chambers to the nearest Underground station. A journey he'd made a thousand times before, and a memory desperately unsettling to Kate's currently fragile peace of mind.

Think of the work around here that needs to be done, she commanded herself. Get outside and start working on the garden. Get some fresh air.

After she consulted and negotiated with the crew working on the restoration of the exterior stone of the North Wing, she spent the next couple of hours vigorously attacking her garden's weeds—pulling, raking, and piling them up with other organic debris into a large mass.

Next, find the bin bags, she decided, as she stood up and stretched her limbs. When she did, her eyes rested on a small stone building set at the farthest corner of her property. She thought she heard music like that of an ancient choir. Maybe the church choir is practicing today, she thought.

This cold, snowy winter has prevented any extensive exploration outside, she realized, and I hardly ventured out at all except as needed to meet with the contractor or run those hooligans off in February.

Walking purposefully now across the garden toward the little stone building, Kate soon stood in front of its ancient-looking wooden door. The door had clearly been unused for a very long time. She reached for its rusty handle.

The door groaned exceedingly when she pulled on the handle. She managed to crack the door open enough to grip it with both hands and widen the gap. The dark interior was unrelieved by any light except what was provided by daylight slanting through the partially opened door. Kate pushed on the door again as far as she dared without risking its coming off its equally rusty hinges. Stepping inside, her first view was obscured by cobwebs and dust.

Kate peered around, her eyes adjusting slowly to the windowless space. The only tools in sight formed an untidy pile on one side of a dilapidated work bench. She decided the bench might be useful and started taking the broken tools off, piling them up near the door.

Since she still had on her leather gloves, she brushed away the debris on top of the work bench. After clearing the heavier dirt, she pulled a kerchief out of her trouser pocket and began wiping away the fine dust that was left. When she did, she saw something carved into the wood of the bench.

Kate stared at the carving, running her fingers over well-worn letters. She closed her eyes and kept moving her finger over the letters until she could comprehend the words — 'an partryk in an peere tre'.

"Oh! That's the beginning of the 12 Days of Christmas — *On the first day of Christmas my true love gave to me, a partridge in a pear tree*. That stands for Christ on the Cross. Some scholars claim the whole song was a secret code for persecuted Catholics after the Reformation. Others that the song was also used as a catechism to teach their children the

Faith. The spelling definitely reflects sixteenth-century orthography. But this bench can't be that old. Is it made up of individual boards or—"

She bent her head down closer and inspected the bench built from individual boards. The carving on this board fully absorbed her attention for some time until her stomach started to growl loudly. Finally, she stepped away and out of the stone shed, dragging the door shut behind her.

"If I were still at the museum, who would I contact?" she wondered aloud as she turned toward the house, her hunger pains becoming more insistent after a tea-only breakfast.

Over a cheese and pickle and more tea, she meditated on the creation of this stone structure.

Was it made from the stones and boards of the convent buildings? Is it really that old or is it only the one board? It could have been built any time after the nunnery was suppressed. After all, the iconoclasts and the subsequent pilferers, carted away whatever was useful to themselves. This stone building is now merely a 'disused tool-shed of respectable proportions.' That's how Saki described the shed where the little boy, Conradin, kept his god the polecat ferret. Saki was asking, whose religion counts and why? The nuns must have been wondering the same.

Dad said the cursing nun was the last prioress of the convent before its dissolution. He also believed her spirit was still confined to this house, grieving and cursing everyone who lived there. Ridiculous. This country is full of supposed hauntings. I once took one of the ghost tours in London. Fun for the tourists but rubbish nonetheless, she scoffed.

Still the thought of an irate, sixteenth-century prioress walking through her house did not help her relax. Kate expelled a singular, staccato breath into the air and headed back outside.

For the rest of the afternoon, she cleared out the broken tools and other debris in the stone shed, checking every piece of any size for more of the 12 Days of Christmas song. She found none.

A hot shower did not dispel the idea or the image of the avenging spirit of a nun ousted by Henry VIII. As she dressed in what she called her "home clothes," flannel pajamas and her faux-lamb lined mules, she tried to redirect her mind to practical matters—eating supper, then sitting in front of the fire, figuring out which projects could be finished before her children returned in two days.

Kate enjoyed cooking but hadn't managed to do much since they moved. Tonight, she found comfort in making a Neapolitan-style puttanesca and adding a glass of Sicilian red wine as the perfect complement. The fragrance of the sauce was heavenly after a day breathing in pollen and dust while puzzling over the words carved in the bench.

Continuing to look for distractions, Kate ate at the table in the kitchen while flipping through the latest museum newsletter from her former London colleagues. In it was a short write-up with a photo of a beautiful eighteenth-century tea box, an artifact she'd always coveted.

I do wish I could find one of these nestled, unnoticed, in a little out-of-the-way antique shop, she mused. Maybe someday. Newsflash: *Yorkshire woman finds 1766 mahogany Chippendale tea box with compartments for two types of tea separated by a bin for sugar. Small key with clover-leaf bow still in lock. Value: Priceless.* Wouldn't that have been something to find in the old stone shed!

But that thought brought her right back to contemplating the partial line carved in the bench as well as the haunting nun. She meant to dispel the image and walked into the sitting room to sit down in front of the fireplace.

"A fire would take the chill off," her nervous energy needing another outlet.

Kate soon had wood and kindling piled onto the grate. When she reached in the small, copper bucket on the floor for the long matches, there were none.

"Maybe there are matches in a nook in this panelling."

She hadn't really begun to explore all the potential nooks and crannies in the old manor house. The interior refurbishing she had done so far concentrated on the most viable and necessary rooms—bedrooms, kitchen, sitting room, toilets. The North Wing was, for now, all exterior work.

The ornate fireplace was a pastiche of sixteenth- and eighteenth-century styles, she thought as she studied it. The fireplace itself simply a recess in the wall of stone, surely sixteenth-century; the oak panelling framing it had all the earmarks of the "finest" eighteenth-century craftsmanship. My ancestors male, from Robert to William Thornton and all their descendants maintained the Old Faith surreptitiously following Henry VIII's draconian *reforms* which included his and his children's bloody executions of anyone who got in their way. Elizabeth I alone executed nearly 200 Catholic missionary priests coming back to England from training in France. That could mean hidden spaces anywhere in the house, couldn't it? Fireplaces like this one were prime locations for such concealed spaces, she remembered.

The hunt for matches receded from her consciousness as she walked around the fireplace running her hand along the surface of the oak panelling. On the far right side, the wood was overlaid with three sets of crossed swords. She stepped back to the front of the fireplace and stared hard at the rectangular piece on the right side of the mantel. Kate recalled photographs of a similar panelling in one of the exhibits she had curated at the museum. That house was in Yorkshire, too.

She went back to exploring the panelling, focusing her efforts on that one rectangle of oak. As her fingers caressed the edges of the wood, she felt metal, shaped like a trigger. When she pulled it, a small door flipped inward. She peered inside, but it was too dark to see anything.

Remember the cat and curiosity, Kate reminded herself.

But, as with the cat, curiosity won out. Kate reached her hand inside, discovering yet another latch. She tugged on that one and heard before she saw the panelling with the swords creak open.

This hasn't been opened in an age, maybe many ages, she thought, as she withdrew her hand from the cavity on the right side of the mantel.

Her arms, a bit sore from her earlier industry in the stone shed, ached with the effort to pull the long-closed door into an open position.

"I don't want to damage this beautiful panelling." The door opened wide enough for her to contemplate entering. "No, I *cannot* go in without a torch." Her voice seemed to wind its way through the open door and into the dark recess beyond.

Kate turned swiftly away from the open panel and went back into the kitchen to fetch a torch, testing its batteries as she returned to the fireplace.

All right, the torch works. Is there anything inside this space, she wondered?

When she stepped through the open door, shining her torch around, all she found at first were more cobwebs and dust. Kate moaned audibly to herself.

Disappointed but not really surprised, she flashed her light over the walls before turning around in the narrow space behind the stone fireplace. As she turned, the torch light reflected off something metallic. She stepped cautiously forward, keeping her beam on the spark of metal. Another latch. This one also resisted the pressure of her fingers before giving way. There was a second recess hidden behind the first.

What is it about this, she wondered, until her memory search found that exhibit of photographs and material from a house in Yorkshire with a priest hide behind the fireplace. This is the same set up. Panelling that opens revealing a space for storing firewood so that the pursuivants would move on to search other parts of the house and grounds. In this hide, the missionary priest or one of the faithful who had smuggled him into the country could be secreted from the government searchers. Did they leave any mass books, vestments, documents?

Excited, Kate stepped carefully into the second cavity, slowly shining her torch on the three brick walls in what was an extremely tight space.

The brick was wide and thick, Elizabethan brick, she realized. The original fireplace built in the earlier part of the sixteenth century had added a priest hide. That would have been constructed by one of a few men who did so in Catholic homes during Elizabeth's reign. Maybe it was even the most sought-after builder of such secret spaces, Nicholas Owen himself! But what a narrow space for a grown man, even then, she reasoned. Someone in a hurry, carrying books or devotional paraphernalia *could* make due here, if his stay didn't extend beyond a day or two.

As she illuminated each wall in turn, she noticed a chink in the mortar around one of the bricks in the third wall. She stepped up closer and ran her fingers over the brick. It felt loose. Pointing her torch at the brick, she held it as steady as possible in one hand while carefully moving the brick back and forth with the other. Finally, the brick slipped out into her hand. Directing her torch light into the void, she spied a small pile of papers with crumbling edges. Her archival training kicked in.

"Don't touch these without proper gloves and a finds' bag," she scolded aloud. Immediately, Kate moved away from the wall, put the brick on the floor, and exited both doors. In the kitchen, she pulled out a pair of cotton gloves and a clear plastic bag. Kate had completely forgotten her search for matches and her fatigue, feeling now only intense excitement. Quick intakes of breath propelled her back to the void in the brick wall.

Positioning her torch toward the wall again, Kate put on the gloves and opened the bag. Reaching into the cavity in the wall, she knew she was reaching across time. Her gloved hand inside, she carefully enclosed the bundle of papers with her fingers and nimbly drew out hand and bundle. She placed the papers tenderly inside the plastic bag.

Kate closed the door to the second space that she now believed without a doubt had been a priest's hide. Then she strode briskly back through the slightly larger opening behind the panelling and closed that door behind her.

She floated rather than walked back to the kitchen table where she laid the bag down on its flat surface. That done, she pulled off the gloves and checked the time on her mobile before calling her friend and former colleague, Dr. Bess Harding.

"Hallo," Bess sounded sleepy.

"Oh, Bess, did I wake you. Sorry." Kate's emotion was obvious.

"Kate? What's happened? Are you in London?"

"Nothing. Something. No, I'm in Yorkshire. But, I want to bring something to you that I've found here. I'll be on the first train out of York in the morning."

"What is it? Nevermind, I know you want to show me first. I'll meet you at King's Cross when your train gets in. Text me the time as soon as you know."

Kate clicked off her mobile and glanced down at the bag full of old papers. She wouldn't expose them to air again but hand the package as is over to Bess who had the facilities to deal properly with such a find. She stared at the papers in the bag for a long time hoping she could discern a date range based on the appearance of the old paper, but it was impossible with the slightly wrinkled plastic between her vision and the artifacts. She left the bag on the table, knowing better than to haul it around any more than necessary.

Kate turned off the lights in the kitchen, glancing vaguely at the unlit wood on the fireplace before extinguishing the lamp in the sitting room. She needed to check train times and text the Farleighs that she would be coming to London on business tomorrow so could meet them somewhere in the late afternoon and take her children back home with her. She knew Peter and Lily would not be happy about the earlier than expected departure. And being fetched by their mother. But she couldn't wait to show them the priest hide behind the fireplace.

After texting Bess the train time, Kate checked her bag for wallet, keys, and other necessaries. Then she extracted her late husband's hard-shell briefcase from under the hall tree seat and went back into the kitchen. She gently lifted the bag of papers from the table and laid the parcel inside the case between two pieces of heavy poster board from Lily's stash. She carried the briefcase back to the hall tree, depositing it into the space beneath the seat, another secret compartment. Then, she climbed up the stairs to her bedroom, hoping to get some sleep before tomorrow's journey.

Rain spattered the windows and a murky grey sky greeted Kate the next morning. Still sitting on the edge of her bed, she picked up her phone when it binged. A text from Lily.

We're having a blast. Don't worry. L

"Lily's phone, but, no doubt, Peter's idea. They are really going to be annoyed with me when they find out I'm taking them home this afternoon. But that annoyance will turn to wonder and delight at what I have to show them."

Kate dressed quickly and ran down the stairs, slowing only long enough to pull the briefcase from the hall tree seat.

When the train pulled out of the York station, Kate sat back in a fairly crowded car but was able to position the briefcase safely on her lap as she watched out the window. Two and a half hours later, she was stepping off the train at King's Cross in London, watching for Bess in the crowd.

When they found each other, Bess instantly peppered Kate with questions. As they walked out of the station, Kate narrated her tale of discovery—a stash of documents that could be letters, sermons, lists of priests. But what exactly and how old, Bess would have to determine.

As Kate expected, her friend was ready to get started unraveling the mystery. By the time they reached University College London off Gower Street, both were practically running for Bess's lab.

Kate had heard from the Farleighs while still on the train and made arrangements to meet them all at King's Cross station at half five. She was mentally preparing herself for the whinging complaints and recriminations about missing their second night in London when Bess exclaimed.

"The one on top is a letter. I'm fairly certain of that, but I can't quite make out the first name of the recipient. The surname is definitely Thornton. See the date on the top left edge of the letter? '8 Feb 1585'."

"But New Style that's 8 February 1586, only a few months before the Babington Plot unraveled, followed by the execution of Mary, Queen of Scots!" Kate's eyes widened as she spoke.

"Kate, this could be an historically significant find, especially if the rest of the letter can be deciphered and is as potentially explosive as this date implies. I'm eager to work my way through the rest of these papers. Naturally, following professional protocols." Bess leaned back and grinned at Kate.

"Oh, my god, I forgot to tell you about the carving on the work bench!"

"What carving, what bench?" Bess asked.

"I checked out this obviously old stone shed in our back garden yesterday to see if I could use it to store gardening stuff. When I was wiping off this rather dilapidated wooden bench in the shed, I found words carved into one of the boards — 'an partrik in an peere tre'."

"Catholic code during the persecutions, right?"

"Yes, a catechism song for teaching the children the tenets of Catholicism. When I realized what the words meant it was thrilling but impossible to trace its origin unless one of my ancestors left a note somewhere, perhaps in there?" Kate pointed to the papers on the lab table and stepped back. "That first paper, the letter, is more significant than I could have imagined. I can't wait to see what the rest hold."

"I'll need more time with them. Can I keep them here, Kate? I'll lock them up, I promise."

"Of course. They'll be safest with you. I'm not, strictly speaking, a conservationist but do know how you work." She looked at the clock on the lab wall. "Must be off to meet Peter and Lily at King's Cross." Her friend started to move. "Stay. I know you're anxious to get started."

With profuse thanks to Bess, Kate left the lab. Rapt in her discovery and future revelations about what it might mean, the twenty plus-minute walk to the rail station felt like a moment. As the chill air of late afternoon touched her face, Kate realized she felt the kind of energy and excitement she thought lost forever after George's death.

I didn't realize how much I missed my work at the museum, she reflected as she walked on toward King's Cross.

Kate wound through the always crowded station. Neither of the Farleighs were tall, but she was sure Peter would be keeping an eagle eye out for her. Five minutes in, she spotted him hopping up and down in an attempt to peer over the crowd.

"MUM!" her son's still high-pitched voice could be heard even over the noise of holiday travelers and commuters.

She waved as she negotiated the crowd, still keeping an eye on her son's bobbing head.

By the time their train pulled into York station, Kate had been privy to an earful, first of the injustice of picking them up early and then of their adventures in the city. She was relieved when they disembarked from the train to wind through another busy station, an action that, momentarily at least, silenced the two children.

Once they were in the car heading home, she found the holiday traffic made the usually quick trip to the village slower and more distracting than usual. Lily and Peter continued alternately to exclaim or to argue about their adventures in London as well as grumble about their mother's abrupt cessation of the same. Kate, trying not to be distracted from her driving, responded with either an 'uh huh' or a brief reprimand. She had her own adventure to impart but would wait until they had eaten and cleared up at home before telling her tale.

After supper, she marched the children into the sitting room and recounted the story of her late-night discovery. When she told them about Bess's initial assessment of the first document, questions erupted from both children at once. And then they proclaimed that they *must* get into the secret spaces behind the fireplace *and* see the carving in the stone shed.

Kate cautioned them to keep their hands to themselves and follow her closely into the recesses behind the fireplace. She promised that they would go out to see the carving first thing in the morning.

By the time their mother announced bedtime, most of the children's questions had been answered. She had no response to Peter's conjecture about a possible priest's ghost in the fireplace cubby (as he and his sister preferred to call it). But all the excitement having taken its toll, the children went on to bed without a fuss.

After she turned their lights out, Kate returned downstairs to warm up by the fire and think about the letter and the potential for the other papers. But, five minutes after Kate put her feet up on the hassock and pulled her grandmother's knitted throw over her, she was sound asleep.

When her grandmother's 1930s' clock chimed the hour, Kate sat up with a start on the final eleventh note. Rubbing the sleep from her eyes, she noticed that the table lamp was still lit.

"It's been a long time since I fell asleep on the sofa so that you could wake me up," she said to the clock. "One of my favorite parts of visiting Nan and Grandad was winding you. I also loved taking trips to

Pontefract Castle where Grandad regaled me with all his historical facts and fictions. Ah, but your a beautiful, old clock still," she said smiling at the clock as at an old friend. "I guess I'd better get to bed before you go off at quarter past, eh, Frenchy?"

She had named the clock the first time she wound it. By then, she was old enough to read the inscription under the number 6, "Made in France," the phrase broken up by an upside down 30 for the half hour, between the words "Made in" and "France."

But Kate was too tired for any more reminiscences. She tossed the throw across the back of the sofa and shuffled toward the staircase, turning the lamp off as she passed the sofa table. The intense darkness stopped her momentarily as her eyes adjusted to the change in light, moonlight creating a chequered pattern on the floor as it streamed through the leaded glass windows into the sitting room.

The weather must have shifted again. It is April, she sighed, before continuing to make her way to the stairs.

In her room, Kate pushed the button on the light switch. The push-button switches were a reminder of her Thornton grandparents, who were the first to have Priory House wired for electricity.

To bed. 'To sleep, perchance to dream. Ay, there's the rub; For in that sleep of death what dreams may come'. I wonder if Hamlet dreamed up his Ghost, she thought, as she drifted off.

Was she dreaming?

A sound like a strangled cry wrenched her from sleep. Kate couldn't tell whether it was real or part of her dreamworld. When the cry came again, it sent a chill through her body and brought her to full consciousness. She decided the sound was only a fox's cry.

That idea took the chill of surprise out but not the chill of the cold room. Kate grabbed the long jumper she kept on the chair by her bed.

"Since I'm awake anyway, I better make sure the screen is up in front of the fire. I'm not certain I put it in place when I came to bed." She was whispering but even that slight sound unsettled her, and the worry about the fire screen nagged her again to get moving.

As she put on her jumper, she reached into the drawer of her nightstand for the torch she kept there. The electricity installed in her grandparents' time, coupled with the old coal-burning power stations in the area being phased out, often resulted in local power failures.

Following the light of her torch down the stairs and into the sitting room, she heard again what she tried to convince herself was a fox crying out for its mate. She shivered.

The moonlight no longer illuminated the floor as she walked through the sitting room, but with her torch, Kate could see the screen sitting at an awkward angle in front of the now nearly extinguished fire.

She adjusted the screen and then reached up to pull the trigger, then the latch in the rectangular panel above the overmantel. The door in the side panel creaked open when she tripped the latch. She wasn't sure why, in the middle of the night, she felt the urge to go back inside the recesses behind the fireplace wall but hesitated only briefly before proceeding.

Shoving the heavy panelled door was a bit easier this time which emboldened her to go on. She regretted not going into the kitchen for a larger torch since her small one lit up the space only a section at a time.

"This will have to do. It's not as if I haven't seen all these cobwebs and dust particles before." Her voice echoed hollowly in the space. She shivered again, swiping at some webs before pulling on the door of the priest hide itself.

The much smaller room, a word perhaps too grand for this tiny space, was better served by the modest torch light. Only then did she notice that she had left the brick on the floor after dislodging it from the wall. Kate bent down, picked up the brick, and slipped it back into the wall. As she did, her torch flashed across the far corner of the space. Her excitement at finding the stash of papers had precluded any more thorough search of the space. On the floor in one corner was something wrapped in faded cloth.

She squatted down next to the bundle and began to unwrap it. It was a book, but not just any book. As she shined her torch on the cover, she realized it was a Douai, the late sixteenth-century Bible of her persecuted ancestors.

Kate nearly dropped her torch as she whirled around to get out of the hide. Running out from behind the fireplace wall, then into and out of the kitchen with cotton gloves and bag in hand, she crashed into the sofa table. Slowing herself down, she went on behind the fireplace and then into the hide to retrieve the bible.

By the time she had the Douai in the plastic bag and laid carefully on the kitchen table, she was breathing heavily, exhilaration and exertion vying for precedence. And her leg hurt where she had hit the table.

"Without a doubt, this is a Douai Bible," she said, shifting her position on the injured leg then gently adjusting the bag to mitigate the glare of the overhead kitchen light.

She stood up and retrieved one of her magnifiers. Returning to the table, magnifier in hand, Kate sat down almost reverently in front of the book.

She pushed the button for the magnifier's light and scanned the somewhat tattered but intact title page: THE NEVV TESTAMENT OF IESVS CHRIST, TRANS-LATED FAITHFVLLY INTO ENGLISH. Keeping the magnifier over the page, she read through the long title, relishing each line.

Following the larger script of the main title was a Latin Vulgate quotation from Psalms 118 accompanied by an English translation of the same. Following that, a quotation from St. Augustine's Tract 2 on 1 John, also with English translation. Below that the printer's colophon: PRINTED IN RHEMES, by Iohn Fogny. 1582. CVM PRIVILEGIO.

"Yes!" Kate nearly shouted. "The *cum privilegio* coming not from the authority of Oxford, Cambridge, or the royal printers for the Bible in England but from the exiled scholars of St. John's College, Oxford, gathered at the English College at Douai, temporarily relocated at Rheims in 1582, during the Catholic diaspora from the English penal laws of Elizabeth I. The religious refugees," her breath gave out.

Kate sat staring at the title page for some time before she roused herself. The clock on the wall across from the table reminded her that she must get back upstairs to grab a few more hours of sleep before the children woke up, raring to go.

And her mother-in-law would be coming for a visit soon. She needed to finish setting up the guest room, Nan's room, as Peter and Lily called it, along with a number of other little jobs that needed doing before she arrived. As Kate struggled to fall asleep, the history of the finds in the priest hide competed with other more personal memories.

She and George moving to London into a cottage in Ealing. Their endless and often ridiculous efforts to keep birds and other creatures from coming through the skylights into the same. The next move to a place large enough for their growing family. George's murder followed quickly by his father's heart attack and his mother's unrelenting grief. Her mother-in-law's stoic but obvious unhappiness when Kate took Peter and Lily to live in Yorkshire. George would have wanted . . . at this, Kate's thoughts trailed off as usual when alighting on memories of her husband. She slept little that night.

Peter and Lily tiptoed into their mother's room at first light, checking her depth of sleep. As they whispered to each other, Kate stirred.

"Yes, my not-so-sneaky ones?" she sat up in bed rubbing her eyes.

"You promised we could go out to the stone shed this morning first thing and then back into the priest's cubby," Lily self-assured, unashamed.

"If you think that's okay, Mum, that we won't spoil any evidence." Peter would definitely be a barrister like his father.

"I found something else last night after a, a fox cry woke me." She still wasn't sure what that sound had been.

A duet of exclamations of various notes followed from the two children standing in the doorway.

"All shall be revealed. Let's go down to the kitchen, and I'll show you what I found before we go outside."

In the kitchen, Kate offered a brief narrative of her second trip to the hide as she pointed to the Douai Bible inside the plastic bag. The children knew not to handle the bag in any way and stood with arms behind their backs listening to their mother's account of its discovery.

"So, after we see the carving in the stone shed, we'll be going back to London today, yes?" Lily always quick off the mark.

"Yes, my dears. Get dressed now so we can make a quick trip outside and then be off. We'll grab something to eat at the train station in York."

The children were off like a shot. Kate dressed quickly and then called Bess. Peter and Lily, standing in front of her again as she clicked off the phone.

"That has to be a new record for getting dressed," their mother exclaimed grinning. The children sprinted to the kitchen door, their mother close behind. After the trip to the stone shed, the morning visit to the hide being forgotten, Kate retrieved George's briefcase from the hall tree and slipped the precious Douai inside. The children raced each other to the car while Kate locked up behind them.

They had just ordered lunch at the Pizza Express across from the British Library when Bess came in to join them.

"Sorry I'm late. Did you order for me?"

"Of course. You and I have shared many meals here so I know your favorites. Hope you're in the mood for Pollo Pesto today," Kate laughed as her friend sat down. Peter and Lily were focused on the sodas, a rare treat, which the waitress placed in front of them. "So, is my Douai genuine?"

"I'm fairly certain it is but will have to contact the expert at the BL for final authentication. A genuine Douai stashed in a priest's hide for more than 400 years and in excellent condition is *quite* unbelievable. The temperature and humidity in there must have been near perfect," Bess said.

"I'm overwhelmed by it all! I don't know what made me go back into the hide when the, uh, fox's cry woke me."

"It was the priest's ghost, mum, not foxes," Lily matter-of-fact as usual.

"That's what I said last night when you showed us the cubby," Peter wanted his share of the credit.

Bess started to laugh but caught herself. She knew better than to laugh at these children's insights. "Peter, a cubby?"

"That's what we call the little room behind the wall of the fireplace. What you and Mum call a priest's hide. It's a cubby-hole, a secret place to read and stash your special treasures."

"That it is," Bess raised her eyebrows at her friend.

Later that day, after some finagling over what one place they could visit in London before they left, the trio were standing in Phyllis Carlyle's mud room taking off their shoes and coats. A visit to the children's Nan was the one place agreeable to all parties.

Although Phyllis later asked them all to spend the night, it was only Lily and Peter who stayed. Kate needed to be at her house in Yorkshire first thing in the morning to meet the contractor and his crew working on the North Wing. She also still had to make some finishing touches on the guest room before her mother-in-law's visit. Phyllis had finally agreed to come up and stay for a bit when she brought the children home later the next day.

That night, on her own again at the house, Kate couldn't keep from revisiting the recesses behind the fireplace—the outer room (the false hide) and the inner room (the actual priest hide).

Well, I can't be disappointed, she told herself when she emerged empty-handed from behind the fireplace. What I've found has been spectacular.

Kate went to the kitchen to put away her large torch and poured herself a glass of wine before settling down on the sofa in the sitting room.

"A small indulgence, Frenchy, given the highly stimulating last two days. Cheers!" Kate raised her glass toward the mantel clock.

As if in response, the clock struck the hour. The sound of the Westminster chime eerily loud in the complete stillness of the house. But the familiar tones and the wine soothed her over-excited brain.

"Who's there?" Kate sat straight up in bed.

What woke her this time was not aural but tactile. A push or a shove on her right shoulder. But no one else was in the house. Or shouldn't be.

This is getting absurd, she exclaimed in her head, avoiding even the sound of her own voice in the room. The chill is the usual one of an old, stone house in late spring. Not ghostly. Surely. Damn. Those two and their priest-ghost fantasy, she frowned.

Wide-awake now, Kate threw the covers back and reached for her jumper, pulling it around her and tying the cloth belt into a soft knot at the front. Then she checked her mobile for the time.

Walking down the stairs, she tried to recall details of the dream she was having when she was so rudely awakened. As she padded in her mules toward the kitchen, the hairs on the back of her neck bristled. She stopped moving and listened.

I'm letting the old curse stories and the children's insistence on a resident ghost get to me. I might as well make a cup of tea with plenty of sugar since it's nearly five.

Again, as if in answer, the mantel clock struck the hour. The tones of the chime hurtling off the mantel through the house. Kate moved on into the kitchen turning lights on as she went.

Still a couple of hours before the workmen arrive and all day before Phyllis comes with the children, she reckoned. *What did wake me up?* Kate's brain felt as if it were echoing the last notes of the chime.

"George. I was dreaming about George. He was trying to wake me up, playful at first, then serious, shaking my shoulder hard. Oh, I hate those mad, too realistic dreams. He was laughing, then frowning, urging me to get up as if something were wrong." Kate slumped down at the kitchen table with her tea cup between her hands, warming, but not comforting her.

Two hours later, she had managed toast and jam with her tea, but she'd hardly moved. A Marimba began to play.

"Hello?" Kate had neglected to look at the caller ID.

"Kate, it's Phyllis, dear, are you awake?"

"Yes, I've been up awhile." She didn't want to say how long or what prompted her out of bed so early.

"Peter and Lily would like to stay over until tomorrow. Is that possible? I promised I'd call you and ask first thing. They're still sleeping, of course."

Kate wondered what special indulgence the children managed to wheedle from their grandmother but also realized that one extra day would give her more time to prepare.

"Of course, Phyllis. What did they talk you into doing today?"

"Wonderful. Thank you, dear. One more day with Nan here in dear London before we trek north tomorrow."

The absence of an answer to her question and the "dear London," recalled her daughter's use of that same phrase before their Easter trip. Kate knew her children were making up for *that* abbreviated visit. Phyllis smoothing it over as usual.

"I'll see you all tomorrow afternoon then." Kate clicked off her phone and sat staring at the black screen. She was still there when she heard the workmen's vehicles arriving.

"I'd better get dressed and walk over to the North Wing for my meeting with the contractor before they get underway today.

At the end of the day, Kate was stacking wood in the fireplace. She laughed at herself when she reached for the matches and found the tin still empty. She hadn't yet replenished the stash on the hearth after her first thrilling discovery.

She retrieved the box of long matches from the kitchen pantry and carried it to the fireplace. Then she struck fire to the tinder. As the flames caught and brightened the hearth, she felt the slight pressure of a hand on her shoulder. She jumped up in a twisting motion to face the room, scattering the matches from the open box across the stone floor.

The light from the still igniting fire barely illuminated the area around her. Her skin prickled and her breath held as she scanned the room in the faint light.

No one's here, she assured herself.

Her mind jangled in time with her nerves, the goosebumps on her arm rising higher. But she bent down and began gathering up the scattered matches. As she placed them in the copper bucket on the hearth, she heard or imagined she heard someone calling out.

"Who's there?" she shouted, her voice echoing in the empty room.

She rushed through the semi-darkness in front of the fireplace to the opposite wall and the light switch. The now well-lit room still revealed no one, no thing.

"What is the matter with me? I've never been excitable or frightened on my own. Maybe I zoned out watching the fire catch, and the changing temperature in the room created the sensation of pressure on my shoulder. And the 'voice' must have been a tawny owl. Their hoot sounds uncannily human sometimes," she struggled for a rational explanation.

But none satisfied. She proceeded turning on lights in each of the downstairs rooms and checked that all the doors and windows were locked. Her apprehension slowly receded with the activity and the artificial light filling the house.

Making herself a small repast revived her a bit more. The commonplace chore of washing up after increased her sangfroid. One more task would secure her peace.

"Bess, it's Kate. I was wondering—"

"Good timing. I was about to call you. Do you have some uninterrupted time right now?"

"The children are in London with their Nan. Coming back tomorrow. What's up?"

"I've managed to decipher more of that first letter although, as always, the rag-based paper has soaked up a good bit of the ink. Under the proper lighting and magnification, I was able to make out roughly the first half of the top sheet."

"What did it say?"

"Here's my transcription so far.

'Honored Sir~ I give you Hearty Thanks for your last letter about the Troubles facing us now. I find some Ancient names omitted in the list you put safely in my hands the last we met. Thogh your family in this county have so far outgone all others having done so Exceedingly much Toward restoring right Majesty to this land. And if it were not, that I should tire out Your patience, I could give you my Conjecture on the outcome of your good efforts: but I know the freedom of your Disposition and right thinking so well that I hope you will pardon my boldness. Our ancient Gentry were so guilty of Henry the 8th sacrilegious robbing the Church, that they mingled Church-Lands with their ancient Inheritances, and 'tis no wonder to see their Children become so corrupted that they in their turn are Issueless. You know

of whom I speak most assuredly. Your progeny, God grant, continues their hopefull promise in spite of the shamelesse Gossippes whose maledictions mock Frenship and your just preservacon of Church-Lands in your Possession.'

Well, Kate, what do you think?"

Silence.

"Kate?"

"My god, Bess. It's extraordinary! And still more to decipher? Did you find the name of the sender anywhere on the fold?"

"No, but, as you well know, that's not unusual for highly vulnerable correspondence during times of political unrest. Certainly was the case for Catholic supporters of Mary in 1586. It's definitely addressed to your ancestor of the period, Robert Thornton."

Bess's excitement matched Kate's, and they talked on for quite some time with Bess promising to email Kate the full transcript. When she hung up, Kate realized the all-engrossing phone call had dispersed the last remnants of supernatural spectres dancing around her.

The next afternoon, the children and their grandmother were duly collected and brought back to Priory House. After setting down backpacks and bags, Kate made the first order of business a show-and-tell of the recesses behind the fireplace. Tour conducted by the children with their mother explicating the discoveries.

"Kate, that's marvelous. Will you be able to keep the papers or will you sell them to the British Library or another archive?" Phyllis Carlyle's own career had been as a special collections librarian in an important London archive.

"Much conservation work has to be done before any decision can be made about relocating the finds, though I'll definitely contact my former Head Curator. My friend, Bess Harding, at UCL's conservation labs, has really just begun to work with the bundle of papers. She sent me a partial transcription of the first item in the bundle via an email last night." Kate pulled up the letter to show Phyllis.

"Wonderful things, as Howard Carter once said." Phyllis's excitement was genuine as she finished reading the transcription.

After supper, the children escorted Phyllis on a tour of their rooms relating the adventure of the intruders from earlier that year as well as the trials and tribulations of their first weeks in Yorkshire. By the time they had finished, Phyllis confessed that she was exhausted and ready for bed.

"Keeping up with those two takes a vast quantity of energy, Phyllis," Kate smiled feelingly at her mother-in-law.

"We hiked all over central London yesterday and then rode the London Eye. Thanks for the extra day with them, Kate."

"Of course. I'm so glad you're here with us now. How long can you stay?"

"I don't want to overstay my welcome, of course, but thought we all could manage a few days, a week?"

"As long as you like, Phyllis, seriously. We love having you."

When Peter and Lily returned to school after the holiday, Phyllis went home to London. She still maintained ties with her former colleagues at the archive where she had worked for three decades. Kate knew that her news would soon be abroad in the archival world.

Soon after, Kate discovered the deceptions of the local contractor she had hired, the one she thought she could count on. The morning of the imagined fox's cry, before the men arrived, she had ventured out to the North Wing with her invoices in hand. Later, as she perused the invoices, the discrepancies in materials and progress on the stonework revealed themselves.

With the help of the Farleighs, she found a solicitor in the village willing to bring fraud charges against the contractor with a little help from Karl, her late husband's barrister friend in London. The solicitor had told her that this type of fraud, "theft or substitution of materials," though high in the UK generally, was usually slightly lower in Yorkshire.

It happened to me in this little Yorkshire village, she had fumed when he told her, "far from the madding crowd" of London.

Her daughter was more pragmatic about it all, "It's the curse, Mum."

"Oh, honey, I don't believe in curses, and you shouldn't either." Kate was in no mood to bring the family curse into a discussion of this case.

"Mum, why else would they cheat us?" Peter. A fair question.

Resigned to the inevitable of allowing the curse into the case of the thieving contractor, Kate launched into her own well-considered hypothesis.

"O.K. let's talk about this. When we moved back here, the village was . . . skeptical about us because of the centuries of rumor-mongering about the so-called nun's curse. At the beginning, some superstitious folks wanted us to be scared off. Remember the teens 'haunting' us when your friends came over the first time?"

Both children nodded their heads to concede the shared memory.

"I think the all-too-human crook, posing as a contractor, figured the curse story provided him a golden opportunity. He could employ sleight of hand with the materials and invoices to rob us with impunity while relying on the legend of the curse if the thefts were discovered. Frankly, he and his accomplices saw me as a gullible, grieving widow who wouldn't question what they were actually doing. They should have known better when I insisted on regular reports of their progress and material invoices every week. I also took my own notes."

Kate scanned the faces of her children. Lily impressed. Peter contemplative.

"That makes total sense, Mum, and now the whole village will know not to mess with us." Lily's smug interpretation.

"Or, that we don't believe in curses or ghosts and are good people. Right, Mum?" Peter the Fair.

"You're both correct, I believe, but I don't want either of you talking about this to any of your friends. You can say 'Phooey' to any curse stories, but that's it until the case against them is over. Remember what your father always said during a case?"

"Keep schtüm." Lily.

"Right. Now, who wants gelato at Roberto's in York?"

Near the end of the summer holidays in late August, Kate stood in her solicitor's office in the village picking up the check for the award granted her against the contractor.

"Thank you so much for all you've done for us in this case. Here's my check for your final bill." Kate wanted all the t's crossed and i's dotted to end this legal fray for good.

"Thank you, Kate. You have been the ideal client. Best of luck finishing your construction project with the new contractor out of York."

"Almost finished, paid for courtesy of the judgment against the crooks." Kate waved her award check and felt a weight lift as she walked out the door of his office down the high street of the village.

Her first stop was the Post Office to deposit her check. After that, she headed for the Farleighs' pub to give them a gift for all of their help and their friendship during these last months.

Kate was meeting Phyllis and the children at the pub as well, Phyllis having moved into Priory House three months before. She told Kate that she believed two strong women would be an immoveable force against all the legal shenanigans that might ensue in Kate's case against the contractor. The two were becoming an enviable team.

She still couldn't bring herself to say the name of the pub, The Nun's Curse, for which the Farleighs had apologized repeatedly over the last months as their friendship grew. But Kate knew the couple needed the business provided by such a name. Despite the charming 'Midsomer' look of the village, tourists were essential to every northern business, especially during the summer. And tourists loved the curse stories. Kate held no grudges for that, especially as everything worked out so well in the end.

The settlement was fair, she considered, and the village contractor is not only in disgrace but soon to be out of business. The new crew from York are finishing the job in record time even though they had to redo a good bit of slap-dash workmanship courtesy of the local crooks.

Yet that summary of events in her head as she walked didn't cover all the good news from the last weeks.

Kate's bundle of papers from the priest hide behind her fireplace had proved not only authentic but historically revelatory, further confirmation of the negative consequences of Henry VIII's sale of monastic lands and the continuity of Catholicism in the county. Kate had secured a dendrologist she knew to test the wood of the bench where the carving had been made. Genuine sixteenth-century oak. All most enlightening for Kate as a scholar and a Thornton.

The final paper that Bess Harding found in Kate's bundle was another letter. This one sent from the last prioress to Kate's ancestor, Robert Thornton, the first owner of the priory lands and buildings at its dissolution in 1538.

The letter revealed that the story of the nun's curse had been fabricated by none other than Robert Thornton himself as a way to keep the locals off the priory grounds in perpetuity, if he was fortunate enough to have surviving issue.

When Kate held the prioress's letter in gloved hands after its conservation, she read the short missive over several times:

Onoryd mayster,

I humbely recommend me to your onorybal self and desyr as alweys your prosperouse helth both bodely and gostely as yow haue always showne yeurself a frend to our house I vnderstande that godds worke and yours wille go togeder when we must be content wt the kynges plesure and leve this hous I would be glad wt all my hart to geve yt In to yeure good handes & trust in youre onest continuying to be oure saluation once we be drevyn oute of this house I offer blessinge vnto yow and all the holy relics of this hous to youre most hygg and prudent wysdome and besech god of hys goodnes to kepe yow in his holy sprete that ye maye do all to hys lawde and glory foreuer.

By hand off your Bedewoman—

Although the signature had been mostly absorbed by the rag paper, enough letters were visible (with the help of Bess's special lights and magnifiers) for comparison with two other letters in a York archive known to belong to the last prioress. The signature was certainly hers.

Kate remembered thinking when she read that letter that this nun believed with full confidence in what Robert Thornton's actions would be after he purchased the priory buildings and lands. She had faith that he would find a way to save their souls by securing their house from the blasphemy (as they saw it) of the new religion. Kate imagined that Robert Thornton misrepresented the prioress's physical departure from the house in such a way that he was able to circulate a rumour about a curse having been performed as she walked away from the priory. That would protect the grounds, he must have reasoned, as well as keeping him and his heirs from suspicion about their religious loyalties. His scheme had worked for centuries.

Kate was certain that the persistence of Catholic practices in her family over several hundred years, in spite of religious persecution, was proof of that interpretation. Even though some of the persecutions her family endured were brought on by her ancestor's fictional curse. Ultimately, all of Robert Thornton's descendants managed to fulfill the prioress's trust.

Satisfied with her mental sorting of the issues, Kate strolled through the pub door just as someone said, "Well, I'm glad she caught 'em. Dirty crooks, preying on a widow woman and her bairns."

That made her smile even brighter as she greeted the Farleighs and her family, ruffling the head of the Staffie puppy, Alfie, that was now part of the family, too. They had fallen for Alfie in a rescue shelter in York a few months before. He was already becoming quite the watchdog and a devoted companion to all.

Phyllis and the children left for London the next day to retrieve the contents of her safe deposit box, and, of course, to have yet another trip to "dear London" before school began the next week. Kate stayed behind to work on a review she was preparing for the latest exhibit in a York museum and, naturally, to care for Alfie.

That night, Kate was filling a glass of water to take up to her bedroom when her old friend, the mantel clock chimed the hour before midnight. She turned off the kitchen light and walked into the sitting room to switch off the lamp on the sofa table.

"Another dark night in the village but not so dark for me any more, Alfie" she patted the pup as the last note sounded.

Alfie already knew the routine so he bounded up the stairs ahead of Kate as she followed more slowly carrying a book and her glass of water.

A few minutes later, Kate lay in her bed, with Alfie across her feet, the lamp on her bedside table positioned over the page of Michael Hodgetts' *Secret Hiding Places*. His book was a source she had read repeatedly but returned to after the discovery of her priest's hide.

Her eyes were heavy after a day getting Phyllis and the children off, finishing her review, and taking Alfie for a long country ramble where squirrels were repeatedly chased though never caught.

Alfie's low growl returned her to full consciousness, the lamp still burning and the book still in her hands though flat on her stomach now.

"Alfie, what is it? Did you hear something?"

Although Alfie was still young and being trained, he had the Staffie's eagerness to please, quickly becoming adept at simple commands—sit, stay, come, walk. And he was turning out to be an excellent watchdog, growl first, bark only when necessary. Alfie was maintaining the low growl as Kate eased out of bed grabbing the torch and her mobile from the bedside table.

"Come, Alfie," she whispered.

As if understanding her caution, Alfie eschewed his usual leaping and quietly slithered off the bed. Alfie in the lead, they walked out of Kate's room and into the long hallway. When they reached the three large windows in the alcove, Kate motioned Alfie to stay while she crossed to peer out of the windows.

No moon shed light on the garden below, and Kate didn't leave the outside flood on any more, as she had for months after discovering the thefts. She could see nothing outside.

"Alfie, I don't think there's anyone out there."

But the dog's hackles were up, and he was still emitting that low growl. He moved quietly but purposefully toward the top of the stairway.

Kate didn't speak to him this time but followed his gaze down the stairs. She couldn't see or hear anything out of the ordinary, only the usual ticking of the mantel clock. Still, she decided to trust this young pup's instincts as they moved in unison down the stairs. The dog stopped abruptly at the bottom, his growl subsiding.

"See, silly dog, no one's bothering us," she stepped over to the sofa table and turned on the lamp.

As she straightened up, she felt the pressure of a hand on her shoulder, patting her gently. She whirled around toward Alfie. He was sitting at the bottom of the stairs regarding Kate expectantly. As suddenly as fear had gripped her, comfort and warmth flooded her system. Alfie came up nudging her hand, his give-me-a-treat move.

"Alfie, what just happened? You were growling, hackles raised. Now, look at you. Cool as a cucumber, wanting a treat." Kate shook her head and motioned Alfie to go back up the stairs.

Halfway up the stairs, the dog stopped abruptly, ears twitching. He heard something that Kate couldn't yet hear. Then she did.

"That's Hildegarde's 'O virtus Sapientie', Alfie. How are we hearing her antiphon? These women's voices singing? How could that be?"

She and Alfie stood transfixed on the stairs, listening to the incandescent voices of women singing the *magistra's* haunting song of the fundamental strength of God's feminine wisdom.

About the Author

In her former life as a professor of medieval and early modern English literature and creative writing, Julie Chappell published six books of scholarship; a collection of her original poetry, *Faultlines* (Village Books Press, 2013); and other scholarly and creative writings. Her poetry and prose have appeared in a number of anthologies and journals including *Cybersoleil: A Literary Journal; Malpaïs Review; Voices de la Luna; Concho River Review; Stone Renga; Speak Your Mind: Woody Guthrie Poets Celebrate Freedom of Speech 2019*; and *Bull Buffalo and Indian Paintbrush (The Poetry of Oklahoma)*. She has also read her work widely in a variety of venues from California to Virginia and places in between. In 1994, she was the Grand Slam Poetry prize winner in Lawrence, Kansas. Since retiring in 2018, she has published two more collections of poetry, *Mad Habits of a Life* (Lamar University Literary Press, 2019) and *As I Pirouette Away* (Turning Plow Press, 2021). Her second collection, *Mad Habits of a Life* was nominated for the Paterson Prize in 2020. Her first collection of original short stories, *Homecoming and Other Mythic Tales*, was published by Fine Dog Press in 2021.